27

PRAYERS OF
A YOUNG MAN

Roch Carrier

translated from the French
by Sheila Fischman

VIKING

VIKING
PUBLISHED BY THE PENGUIN GROUP
Penguin Books Canada Ltd, 10 Alcorn Avenue, Toronto, Ontario, Canada M4V 3B2
Penguin Books Ltd, 27 Wrights Lane, London W8 5TZ, England
Penguin Putnam Inc., 375 Hudson Street, New York, New York 10014, U.S.A.
Penguin Books Australia Ltd, Ringwood, Victoria, Australia
Penguin Books (NZ) Ltd, CNR Rosedale and Airborne Roads, Albany, Auckland
1310, New Zealand

Penguin Books Ltd, Registered Offices: Harmondsworth, Middlesex, England

First published 1999

1   3   5   7   9   10   8   6   4   2

Copyright © 1998
Les éditions internationales Alain Stanké
English translation copyright © Sheila Fischman, 1999

*Publisher's note: This book is a work of fiction. Names, characters, places and incidents
either are the product of the author's imagination or are used fictitiously, and any
resemblance to actual persons living or dead, events or locales is entirely coincidental.*

Printed and bound in Canada on acid-free paper ∞

CANADIAN CATALOGUING IN PUBLICATION DATA

Carrier, Roch, 1937–
[Prières d'un adolescent très très sage. English]
Prayers of a young man

Translation of Prières d'un adolescent très très sage.
ISBN 0-670-88587-8

1. Fischman, Sheila. I. Title. II. Title: Prières d'un adolescent très très sage.
English.

PS8505.A77P7313 1999   C843'.54   C99-931240-5
PQ3919.2.C25P7313 1999

Visit Penguin Canada's Website at **www.penguin.ca**

Other works by Roch Carrier
available from Penguin Books Canada

Prayers of a Very Wise Child
Heartbreaks along the Way
The Man in the Closet
The End
The Lament of Charlie Longsong

Contents

PRAYERS OF
A YOUNG MAN

Prayer of a Child
Whose Big Trunk
Is on the Roof of the Car

Dear God, please look at me. I'm eleven years old and I'm leaving our house, our parents, our brothers and our sister. They're all with me now, piled into our black Ford with my big trunk fastened to the roof. Our house is staying behind, where it was built. In my nostrils there is still the aroma of juicy meat that was cooked with carrots, onions and pepper. I'm thinking about our bedroom: through the window, on the other side of the forest and the other side of the American border, if the weather's not too bad, you can just see the lights of the city of New York. Some people think it's not New York. In our family, only our father's eyes are good enough to make out the skyscrapers that are all lit up. And I can see as well as our father.

As for my squirrel, he's staying behind in his

cage. He has to keep turning and turning on his wheel like a soul in Hell. I explained to him that I'm going away to the Petit Séminaire to get an education. I think I heard him say: "Good luck." I wouldn't tell anyone but You that, God. I gave him three handfuls of hazelnuts. I wouldn't want him to forget me. After that I tried to stroke his head. He bit my finger. I have a bandage. He didn't want me to forget him.

Through the back window of the Ford, I watch as our house moves away. The big willow where it hides its nose seems to be quietly following us. We've driven past the house of our grandmother, who insisted on being there for her grandson's departure. I'm going away now just as her sons, my uncles, did when they were my age. She says herself that her memory is like a sieve. She wasn't outside on the street. She must have forgotten that I'm going to the Petit Séminaire today. Our father blew his horn to let her know, but she's a little deaf.

The church steeple on the hill seems to be following us too. I think, I'll never ring the bells in the village church again. Our grandfather, who's the beadle, is going to replace me with our brother. I won't pull the ropes any more. Even though I'd got the bells to obey me. I made them sing like the children in the choir. It won't be the same with our brother. He's too young to look after the bells as well as I did. Noon and night, at every wedding, every christening, every funeral, the people will hear that the bells aren't singing the same song.

Then, as we were driving along the gravel road, a cloud of dust swirled up just like a sandstorm in the desert. The place where I was born disappeared. I'll be coming home for the Christmas holidays. When a person returns it's not the same as if they had stayed. I've listened to people who'd come back to the village. They all said: "When you've been away, it's different." You have to go away again.

I fall silent. I keep my chin down on my chest, but I bet You anything, God, that I won't cry. Take a good look at me. Can You detect even one tear caught in my eyelashes? Our father told us that he didn't cry either when he left his parents' house. He was eleven years old, like me, but he was going away to fell trees in the forest. At home we have a yellowing photo stuck in the album that's in a dresser drawer in our parents' bedroom: there's a cabin made of logs that still have their bark, which is where he slept, on a bed made of fir boughs. In front of the cabin stand two rows of proud, strong lumberjacks with axes and moustaches and their chests sticking out. Our father is in the front row. He holds his axe like the men, he sticks his chest out like the men, but he doesn't have a beard. Just a pipe.

Dear God, I hate the smell of tobacco. Whenever our father smokes in our Ford, I choke. And he always smokes. We aren't allowed to open the windows. He complains that the smell of grass and flowers makes him cough. So we're prisoners in the black Ford. Our father lights one cigarette after another. There's so much smoke we can't see one another. Our father coughs. When he isn't coughing, he complains that the letters on the road signs are as small as the print on a notary's contracts.

I'll never become a lumberjack like our father. I'll never cut down one of Your trees, God, except for a fir tree at Christmas time. Farewell house, farewell school, farewell baseball diamond, farewell cow pasture! Farewell spruce forest where the hares laugh when they see me setting out snares. Farewell Quamme River where the trout will miss the fat squirming worms I offer them! I'm going to where the books are that you have to read so you can learn everything you need to know if you want to go far along the road of life.

When he was eleven, our grandfather also turned his back on the family house. His hat was too big for his head, which was still so small. The wind snatched it away from him as if it were a bad schoolboy who wanted to make him suffer a little. Also too big were his boots, which hurt his feet. When I asked him if he'd cried when he left his father's house, he told me: "There were two or three babies in the house. When you're

5

Prayer of a
Child Whose
Big Trunk Is
on the Roof
of the Car

eleven years old, you're a man. And as a man, I was responsible for helping my family. Do you think my crying would have put bread on my father's table?"

My eyes are dry, like my father's and my grandfather's. In spite of that, though, I can't promise You, God, that I won't shed any tears when our father, our mother, our brothers and our sister leave me all alone at the Petit Séminaire with my big trunk. I don't know yet what I'll think about when the black Ford turns its back on me and drives away. Will I think about our mother's delicious strawberry pies? Will I think about my bed under the quilt and about the wonderful pillow fights with our brothers? Will I think about my friends who aren't going back to school, who've promised themselves that as long as they live, they'll never open another book because they already suffered so much when they learned how to read and write? Will I think about old man Albert's hill, where it was so good to stretch out in the grass and watch the train go by, with the names of far-off countries painted on the cars? Will I think about my *Encyclopédie de la jeunesse?* Those books are packed with wonderful stories from the olden days. They're also crammed with clever things you have to know if you want to understand other clever things. When our family leaves me, that's when I'll decide if it's worth the trouble of letting some tears wet my eyes.

I'm eleven years old and I'm abandoning the place where I was born. I'm not crying, but I do have a lump in my throat. My heart doesn't feel like beating the way that it usually does. I'm going away like my cousins who emigrated to New York when they were my age. The only thing they knew about that city was that it has more streets than all the towns in the province of Quebec put together. They also knew that they couldn't understand the English language that was spoken in the city. To show that they were men, they did their best to keep their eyes dry in the bus that was taking them away. They bragged that they'd come back driving a long American car with lots of chrome, dressed in a fine American suit, with a watch and a tooth both made of gold. They were also looking forward to putting beautiful American dollars into an envelope and mailing them to their family so they could buy necessary things and even oranges.

As for my uncles who studied at the Petit Séminaire, they won't say whether they cried when they left home. Like them, I'll come back with a trunk filled with books. I'm going to explain to our brothers and our sister what is written in those books, because I'll have read them all, even the big, thick one that provides the nine proofs of Your existence, God. I want to learn everything that is known. I want to understand the mysteries of Your creation, the universal history of all the peoples on Earth, Your Bible, chemistry, geography, French grammar and all its exceptions, Latin, Greek and even English. I want to go far along the road of life. Then, when I've gone far enough, I'm going to decide to become Prime Minister of Canada. My father will be glad. Will You vote for me, God?

A long time ago, on the day when I started going to school, our father told me: "Education is a Station of the Cross. But it's not worth putting up with so much suffering unless, at the end of the road, you become the Prime Minister of Canada." God, You'll make my father so happy if You elect me Prime Minister! That won't be for quite a few years. Will our father still be alive to see it? And if he's not dead, will his ears still be good enough to hear my speeches?

If I'm not chosen to be Prime Minister, I want to become an inventor. I'd like to find a way to make a magic pencil so that, when I write the name of a country, I'll be transported there right away, at the speed of light . . . or sound. Which one travels faster, God, light or sound? I can't wait to devour the books a person has to read to understand science! Do You want to know how my invention works, God? Let's say I'm at home, eating soup. All at once I think that I'd like to visit the Druzes, in Serba. That's a city in Lebanon, as it says on page 307 of volume III of *Pays et nations*. I'd just pick up my

9

Prayer of a
Child Whose
Big Trunk Is
on the Roof
of the Car

magic pencil and write the word *Druzes*. Immediately, I'd arrive in the place where those people who practise a secret religion live. It's so secret, You might not even know it Yourself. And then I'd invent another pencil that would have the power to place me in another era. For instance, I could take my magic pencil and write: "The year 16937." And bingo, there I'd be, among the people of the future. God, I just hope the Petit Séminaire will have the necessary books. I want to learn everything you have to know to invent everything I want to invent. But if I can't create an invention, then I'll become Prime Minister, which is what our father wants.

God, I'm going to stop praying to You because I can see the dome of the Petit Séminaire on the hill. Our house and the place where I was born are far behind me, already in the past. It feels as if I'm going to cry. I am standing and facing the future. I'm choking as if I'd swallowed a stone.

If it is Your will, I'm ready to cry like a rainy day, but first I'd rather say goodbye like a man to our father, our mother, our brothers and our sister.

Please help me, God. This is Your little boy's first step along the road of life and I want to go far.

11

Prayer of a
Child Whose
Big Trunk Is
on the Roof
of the Car

2

Swearwords
Prayer

Wash my mouth out with soap, God, I beg You.
I absolutely have to pray to You because my lips
have come out with some very bad words. Only
a man with lots of hair on his stomach can say
them without getting goose pimples. Since it
was You who created me, You know that I'm
only eleven years old and I haven't got even the
first hair of a beard. Even so, I swore like a grown
man. I'm going to confess to the priest because I
don't want to be cast into Hell. I'm pretending
to be calm, but I'm quaking with fright in my
student uniform that's already too tight for me,
even though it was quite a bit too big when our
mother bought it.

You heard them, God; those swearwords were
intended to shake up Your eardrums. Have pity
on me! I profaned the sacred vessels of Your

priest. I insulted the holy name of Your blessed mother. Forgive Your child who talked the way real men in Dorchester County talk. Please, God, don't let our train be derailed. It's my first trip.

Oh, I know, we're not supposed to let ourselves repeat the swearwords we hear. I only wanted to show that I wasn't afraid of them, even if they were stronger than the engine of the train. Only You know how scared I was. I'm sure You're angry at me. I beg You, God, please, overlook my insults. If You wanted to, You could flick a divine finger at our train and it would fall off the bridge. I don't know the name of the river underneath. It would make a wonderful disaster photo for the newspaper. Don't punish me right away. Hold back Your divine anger. A well-behaved boy's prayer should cancel out a few swearwords. The ones I said were bad enough to take years of prayers to atone for.

For a long time I've dreamed about sitting in a train to take a trip. Do You remember, God? I'd lie in the field that's smeared with red strawberries and white daisies, up on old man Albert's hill. While I waited for the train to show up, down below, in the valley, I would look up at Your sky. I tried so hard to get a glimpse of You through the blue of the sky! I was dazed. I'd have liked so much to get even one little look at You. I was expectant, like the audience as it waits for the magician behind the curtain that shivers before the show begins. I forget that You're invisible. But God shouldn't always hide Himself. Earthlings won't want to go on believing in Your existence if they never get to see the tip of Your nose.

Gazing so hard at Your sky made me dizzy. I was dazzled by Your mystery. The clouds were racing like a flock of white sheep. Earth was rolling along like a big flowery balloon. And I was sneezing because of the rough perfume of the grass. I closed my eyes. I would have been happy if I could have understood Your mystery. I sensed the ecstasy the birds must feel when they soar between earth and sky. I was happy I'd been born. I was happy to be a child. I thought that without You, God, I'd never have been created. I didn't want to become an adult. In our village, the men and women aren't very happy. I wanted to see the whole world, but I wanted to remain a child. All at once, the leaves on the poplars were stirred by a gentle quivering. The train was whistling in the forest. The clouds were slowing down. The earth was stopping. The train sped into the valley. Its bell rang out like the school bell on mornings when the nun was impatient. The engine was gasping. The chimney was exhaling white smoke. And I was observing everything that was going on. How happy I was to be able to admire so many marvels in my life! The cars streamed by and on their sides I could read strange names that sounded like magic formulas: *New Mexico, Pacific Railway, Pennsylvania, California*. Then I started to run as if I could catch the train . . . It was too far away and I didn't really want to catch it. I wasn't ready to leave yet . . . Later . . . Some day, I would board the train . . .

Today, I really was travelling on a train. I was going back to my family for Christmas. I was separated from our house, our mother, our father, our brothers and our sister a hundred and eleven days ago. That was longer than the four thousand years in the song about waiting for the Messiah. It was last September. Since then, I haven't been outside of my Petit Séminaire. I'm learning Latin. That's the language You understand best, God, so they tell us. Have You forgotten Your Hebrew, God, the way the French Canadians in the United States have forgotten their mother tongue? I've learned how to say "Merry Christmas!" in Latin. Our father will be proud of my education. The only danger was that I might forget how to say it during my journey on the train.

The fir trees looked as if they knew it was Christmas time. They were decorated with glittering snow like you see on Christmas cards. We watched them speed by all down the length of the train, and our heads were spinning.

Along with me, two other boarders were also going home for the holidays. We didn't talk to each other very much. We were too anxious to be back in our own houses. Each of us was thinking about the life we hadn't lived while we were at the Petit Séminaire. Even though we were in the train, each of us was already back at his house, at home. Each of us was already breathing in the aroma of the soup steaming on the table, which was covered with a cloth in honour of our return. All three of us were wearing our school uniforms. All three of our uniforms were a little tight. We'd grown a fair amount since September. One of us even has a dusting of moustache, but only under his left nostril.

Across the aisle in our car, two bearded men were passing a green bottle back and forth. They were drinking strong alcohol. They were telling each other the stories told by robust men who work in the forest. Their voices were rough. When they laughed, it was practically like thunder when it rolls down the mountains. We had just spent four months with Your priests who wear black dresses like nuns and who talk daintily, with the tips of their tongues, like the angels in Your heavenly choir. For a hundred and eleven days we hadn't heard men talk like men. The two lumberjacks were conversing in loud voices as if they were deep in the forest, overcome by the silence of the trees. Instead of commas in their sentences, there were swear-words. They were cursing the name of Your blessed mother and all the sacred objects that are used to celebrate Your holy sacraments. We didn't dare plug our ears. We listened to their blasphemy the way people look when they know they're not supposed to.

All at once the bigger of the bearded lumber-jacks turned his black eyes to us, the three schoolboys. He studied us the way he probably stares at a tree before he strikes it with his axe. After a moment's reflection, he proclaimed in his muscular voice:

"You're little students, right?"

All three of us replied together:

"Yes, Monsieur."

"Students are nothing but little twigs of men."

All three of us sank into our seat. It was a wooden bench because the car is an antique from before World War I.

The other bearded man was thinner, but taller. His voice rang out even louder:

"Them students, they wear little ties and little pressed pants. They got good manners. They been brought up right."

"Not like us. Us, we're foul-mouthed drunks."

"They're educated. They don't have to earn their bread by the sweat of their brow even in the winter."

"They know how to behave. You'll never hear a curse word out of them."

"Them little altar boys, except for praying they'd never say their Saviour's name out loud."

"They got so much education they've forgot how real people talk."

"They're scared of real people."

The thinner bearded man took a slug from his bottle, stowed it between his knees, gave us another good look and concluded:

"They got too much education to talk to lumberjacks like us. Us, we drink booze and fart swearwords."

What they were saying must have been very

funny. The two drinkers were laughing, with their heads on each other's shoulders, and they were slapping their thighs with their big hairy hands.

"Look at them little students—they're scared of us when we talk to them."

I was the youngest. God, I felt more uncomfortable than if I'd been sitting at the front of the class. The bigger bearded man was checking me out. Under his bushy eyebrows, his black eyes were filled with scorn as if I were a cockroach. After another long slug he announced to us:

"Inside your educated little pants you're shit-scared."

(Excuse me, God, I know *shit* is a vulgar word. Luckily, You don't have to think about that mortal imperfection.)

I pulled myself away from the lumberjack's terrible gaze and I felt as strong as Superman when I realized that I was saying:

"I'm not scared!"

The thinner bearded man repeated:

"You aren't scared?"

"No, I'm not!"

God, I'd never been so scared in my life.

"You aren't afraid to say swearwords?"

I was so afraid, God, that I lied:

"No, I'm not afraid to say swearwords."

"But I bet you're scared to say swearwords like I do," suggested the bigger bearded man.

"I am not."

"Okay, if that's so, repeat what I'm going to say, like a man."

The lumberjack launched a burst of shocking profanities. The floor of Your Heaven must have shaken. If You didn't hear it, God, Your ears must be going be a little deaf.

I repeated what he'd said, word for word. I ask You to forgive me. I hate blasphemy. I didn't want to commit a sin. I didn't want to soil the names of the holy objects in Your church. I was just trying to show those lumberjacks that the students of the Petit Séminaire aren't wimps. Absolve my sin, which may be mortal. Have pity on me. I didn't want the lumberjacks to know that we were scared.

At the Petit Séminaire we learn how to be useful to our people. Can we be useful to our people if they think we're afraid of the words of a couple of lumberjacks? Yes, I was scared. And I'm even more scared now because I repeated those forbidden oaths. Please, God, don't punish Your child who is praying to You right after he committed his sin. Don't derail our train to punish me. Don't order the earth to open up and swallow us in the flames of Hell, along with the lumberjacks. I'm nothing but a little seminarian. I haven't smelled the aroma of our mother's soup for a hundred and eleven days. I'm looking forward to celebrating Christmas, Your holiday.

After he'd heard me blaspheme the name of Your blessed mother, Your blessed father, Your blessed sacraments and Your sacred objects, the bigger bearded man said to me:

"Okay, maybe you aren't afraid to curse like a man . . . but we're pretty sure you're scared to drink like a man. You got too much education to drink like a lumberjack that hasn't got any education but he's got blisters all over his hands."

I declared:

"I'm not afraid to drink like a man."

He passed me his bottle. I took three sips. I ask You to forgive me for that, too, God. It tasted like gasoline. It burned my stomach. A few seconds later I had ideas turning around in my head like birds with their asses on fire. (Forgive me that vulgar word. Your priests still have a ways to go before my language is civilized.)

God, I don't know if You've ever travelled on a train, but a man mustn't be scared in this life. Amen.

3

Prayer for Snow Falling on the Rink

Once again our village is all decorated with lights for the Christmas celebrations. I've got quite a lot older since last year. I notice that the girls' cheeks are tantalizing now. The winter drops cold kisses on them. Didn't I put that well, God? Inside their parkas they've also got beautiful round bumps that You gave them in exactly the right place.

Do You know where our rink is? Long ago You spread the new December snow. In the clear blue night of our severe cold snaps, You must be able to see Your rink shining under the floodlights. Are You interested in what Your children are doing here on earth? If You are, You must glance now and then at the pocket of ice that's not very far from Your church.

I expect You've got other things to do

though. In fact, I'm tempted to say that if You spend all Your time spying on teenagers at the rink in their village, it could explain why so many things turn out so badly in this world. Excuse me for speaking to You the way a man speaks to another man. At thirteen, a person's beginning to think about what the writer Malraux called the human condition. The librarian told me that his book is too advanced for me.

At the rink, we play till half past eight at night and sometimes as late as nine. That's when our mothers expect us. We're supposed to go home. To begin with, we boys grab the puck from one another, we fight over it, we shove one another, we squabble. That's hockey. The girls gather around the rink in their coloured parkas. Their white skates hang over their shoulders by the laces. Just admiring the boys, they have even more fun than we do. Otherwise they wouldn't stand there, at twenty below with the wind from the north, their boots in the snow, their noses white with frost and their cheeks red. We're males, so we attract females. It's normal, it's one of the laws of nature that You've promulgated.

The puck slaps against the blades of our skates. The girls go into ecstasies if one of us scores a goal. Why can I never shoot the puck into the net? Do You really want me to be a bad hockey player, God? Why is it that You planted in my head the desire to become a great champion like Maurice Richard, who scored his first hat trick on December 31, 1943?

My life would be nicer if the girls noticed that I'm part of the team too. When the puck glides towards me, God, wouldn't you sometimes like to inject Yourself into my arms and legs, to skate in my body, and drive the puck into the net at the speed of light? The girls' shouting would be as loud as the singers in Your choir at Sunday mass. The triumph would be a balm to the private torments of Your former altar boy, who never manages to score a goal . . .

During our hockey game, You all at once activated a heavy snowfall. It was as if You'd ripped open Your pillow and spread the white goose feathers over the earth. By the end of the game, the snow was so thick that we sank into it halfway up our thighs. We all decided to clear the snow from the ice.

The girls came onto the rink armed with shovels, like the boys. Together, we tackled the storm. They tried to lift shovelfuls as big as ours. The girls aren't as strong as we are, but they're prouder.

Somebody, probably one of the big boys, put "The Skaters' Waltz" on the record player. The girls laid down their shovels, laced on their skates and rushed onto the ice. In their parkas, with their hoods on their heads, they looked like brightly coloured flowers, if You understand what I'm saying. Slowly, the boys began skating too.

Me, I didn't stop shovelling. As long as there was still some snow on the ice, the work wasn't finished. The snow had a perfume, I can't exactly describe it, a perfume of angels' wings. The night smelled good too. Its odour didn't make you make a face the way the women's perfume does at mass on Sunday. It was a nice smell, like the smell of the Quamme River. The air was stretched tight like the string of a violin. We could sense that the night was fragile. Tell me, God, where do I get expressions like that? Could it be that I've come down with a case of poetry instead of the mumps?

After "The Skaters' Waltz," they played "The Blue Danube." I don't know what vitamin is in that music. When I hear it my heart starts waltzing in my chest. The boys and the girls were skating together. Each boy had his girl. Each girl had her boy. They were whirling around the rink like my squirrel on his wheel. And I was shovelling snow. I'd never skated with a girl, but I knew what you have to do. First of all, you have to agree to go at the same speed. After that, the girl has to let you hold her by the waist. The two right feet and the two left feet—each in turn—have to move together, otherwise the two skaters will trip and fall. The two right skates and the two left skates, each in turn, have to touch the ice at the same moment. They have to glide the same distance at the same time. With every movement, the boy and the girl have to give a push of identical force. What's most complicated is holding the girl's waist in your arm. Boys are ready to do very complicated things for girls.

Your knowledge is infinite, God, but I know more about skating with girls than You do. I've been studying the subject for several years. Getting ready. The great event would occur one day, I knew it. I too was going to skate with a girl. And if I committed the sin of having too much fun skating with her, I'd confess it after the holidays, back at the Petit Séminaire.

In the meantime, I was shovelling snow while the others were skating. I wasn't happy. Why was I all alone? You didn't create me so I could shovel snow while the other boys were skating with the girls as if they were dancing on the beautiful blue water of the Danube.

I was watching. The flowers that sway on their stems in the meadows may be more beautiful in the sunlight, but the girls are more beautiful under the veil of night. Are You listening to me, God? Should I become a great poet instead of Prime Minister?

All the players on our team and even the ones on the enemy team had a girl clinging to their arms. While I was holding a shovel! Now it's true, the others play hockey better than I do. At the Petit Séminaire, I've had my nose stuck in a book for months. They stay in the village; they've got nothing to do except make the girls notice them. While I'm learning Your Latin. Maybe girls aren't attracted by Latin. Another thing they don't like is the pimples that are stuck in my chin like nails!

Whatever the reason was, I was alone. The others were holding a girl close to them. They looked as if they'd discovered happiness on earth. Would I always be alone in the world, with my shovel, at one end of the skating rink, looking at an acre of snow that had to be cleared?

Why had I been abandoned? I've been chosen by the authorities of the Petit Séminaire as a future member of the elite of our French-Canadian people. I'm going to become Prime

Minister, or a great inventor, or a famous poet. I shouldn't have been neglected. If there was justice on Your earth, the girls would have fought each other to waltz across the ice with me. Now, I'm learning Virgil's Latin! And the Greek of Aristophanes! Why do the girls prefer those lumberjacks, those truck drivers, those chicken farmers?

I'm sure You remember that I said a prayer just then. I said to You: "Make me into a lumberjack if that's what I need to skate with a girl." I also told You: "If You're fair, if You love all Your children equally, it seems to me that I deserve a girl."

I started shovelling again, like a convict. If the girls could see me at work, maybe they'd realize that I exist! The snow smelled good. Its white scent was making my head spin. Or was it the music of "The Blue Danube"?

All at once, Claire appeared. Her parka was sky blue. Her blond hair was spread across her shoulders like golden wheat on the western plains. She was the most beautiful girl in the village school. Since I've been away, she's become even more beautiful. Claire skates like a ballet dancer. I saw one in a movie once, but never in real life.

Claire didn't have a hockey player clinging to her yet. I made a decision. I said to myself: "I'm going to grab hold of the beautiful Claire!"

I dropped my shovel. I shot towards Claire like Maurice Richard heading for the net. Claire was so beautiful! Her smile, her blue eyes, her blond hair, her parka with the bumps on the chest: I was blinded. I couldn't apply the brakes. We had a collision, with sparks. Claire took a tumble, her face landed on the blue line. I collapsed onto her. I tried to pick myself up as quickly as I could, but I had enough time to breathe in her smell, that was like candy. My nose was in her hair. My chest felt the round hardness of hers. I heard her blaming me: "You idiot!"

I got ninety-nine out of a hundred in mathematics. If Claire had known that, she'd have been proud of a Pythagoras on skates.

God, I ask You to forgive me for being called an idiot. If Claire is right, only You who created me have the power to make me over differently. Will I skate with a girl some day, to the tune of "The Blue Danube," under Your starry sky?

Roch
Carrier

4

Prayer of the Woman in the Television

For a few days now we've had both feet firmly in the year 1950. I'm looking at the greatest invention of our century. Television is a much better thing than the atomic bomb. Now when we want to amuse ourselves, we don't have to go out into the icy January air. Why should we go outside and freeze our ears and our brains? We men stay snug and warm inside, in the heat that smells of french fries at the Chez Viateur restaurant. Let the girls go skating by themselves! Let them freeze their cheeks, the ones on top and the ones down below! We men are watching television without them.

You invented everything in the world, God, so You must have television in Your house. We on Earth had a fairly long wait for that brilliant invention. Television was already in the comics, along with interplanetary travel, but all my life, even when I'm an old man of fifty, I'll remember that I watched television for the first time when I was thirteen, in 1950. In our village there's just one television set. The first one. One set, just as there is one God. And I've seen it. Thanks to You, God, whom I haven't seen yet.

My friends at the Petit Séminaire don't know yet what it's like to watch television. Thank You, God, for granting me the grace of television. At Chez Viateur, we settle into the cloud of tobacco smoke, we sprinkle vinegar onto our golden fries, and we chomp away while we watch the screen. The only people who dare to talk are those who've earned everyone else's respect because of their experience in life. The rest keep quiet. Mouths shut, eyes glued to the screen. We don't look at anything else. Every now and then a girl walks by on the street. We don't allow ourselves to be disturbed. No one even bothers to look at her. We men are gazing at the greatest invention of this great twentieth century which will end fifty years from now,

when I'm dead and buried in our planet's earth.
(Will You invite me into Your Heaven?)

Since it has no screen, we can predict that
the radio is going to become a useless invention.
In the atomic age, what earthly use is an old
invention without a screen?

We men hang around in front of the television set for hours. All we can see is snow.
They're supposed to give us pictures to look at.
A blizzard. There's as much snow on the screen
as in our fields. But we stick with the television.
For days now, we men have been watching the
snow fall. The television revolution is more
important than the French Revolution! A number of people have already decided to get rid of
their radios.

Gusts of snow are swirling on the screen just
like the real snow outside Chez Viateur's window: no picture. No sound either. The snow on
the television is as silent as real snow. We see
nothing, we hear nothing—but we know that
what we're looking at is the greatest invention
of the twentieth century.

We're the first to find ourselves face to face with television. We're like the men who were the first to see a plane fly. We're admiring what we see. Our mothers and sisters back at the house haven't seen what we see. I, like the famous French philosophers, am reflecting on the progress of humankind.

Tonight, gathered in front of the television at Chez Viateur, we men were watching the snow, listening to it fall. Outside Chez Viateur's window, fleecy white snow was dancing; the women and girls, muffled in their furs and scarves, were on their way to the church, already bowed down in prayer. We men were staying in front of the television set.

All at once the door was flung open by a black gust of wind. Your curé's soutane appeared, and his fur hat, which was dotted with snowflakes too.

We men didn't fling ourselves to our knees as tradition demands. We know that Your curé represents You here on earth, just as the local MP represents the Prime Minister, but we were busy watching television.

So Your curé proclaimed:

"Get moving, men! Your wives and daughters are already in church. They've already started their prayers. It's time for you to come and kneel with them and sing the vespers of the Lord."

"*Monsieur le curé*, you can see that we're busy with the television," explained the bank manager, who is also the choirmaster in the church choir.

No one took his eyes off the screen. Your curé was shaken by a volcanic rage. Our lack of piety was mocking his divine authority.

Like a saint, he held back his reproaches. Instead of threatening to send the Devil to pull our ears at night, instead of predicting the birth of two-headed calves and club-footed children, instead of prophesying that we were going to be flung into the flames of Purgatory, instead of upbraiding us for making Your blessed mother weep, instead of warning us about Your vengeance, your curé didn't say a word. We could tell that he was thinking very hard. He didn't even let out a sigh. And he started watching the television. Your curé was with us. Like us, he was probably thinking that television's a lot more interesting than church.

After a few moments of silence, Your curé turned to me:

"You, young man, the good Lord has chosen you to become a guide for our people. You're going to come along with me and pray for those who refuse to pray. We're going to ask God to protect our people from the dangers that are threatening their future."

After thinking it over, I replied:

"*Monsieur le curé*, I've prayed so much since I've been at the Petit Séminaire, the good Lord must be tired of listening to me."

As if he'd been spurred by a wasp, even though it's winter and the wasps are all asleep, Your curé started delivering a sermon.

"My dear parishioners, the heart of the Sacred Heart of Jesus is bleeding because of your ingratitude and your paganism... sweet Saviour! I beg You, do not send the ten plagues of Egypt to our village. Give Your humble curé a chance, just one chance, as You would give to one of Your Righteous, to gather up your flock who've lost their way on the path to Your church, where we're going to sing vespers."

"*Monsieur le curé*," suggested Chauve's son, "you ought to put a television set in the church!"

Your curé swept outside like another gust of wind. The snow kept falling on the other side of Chez Viateur's window. He went back up towards the church, bowed down by the wind and his responsibilities.

We men felt proud. We felt strong. We hadn't been afraid to disobey Your curé. For the first time since white men arrived in our village, we hadn't listened to the curé. If ever a revolution should break out in the province of Quebec, I'm telling You, God, it will have started today, when we men told Your curé that we preferred television to his prayers.

Outside, the snow was piling up on the balconies and staircases. I was watching the snow on the screen. That snow, I wouldn't have to shovel.

It was a little later that the miracle occurred. Yes, God, a miracle. All at once the snow on the screen opened like a theatre curtain. A face appeared, the face of one of Your angels in paradise: an angel who looked like a beautiful woman with curly blond hair. Hair doesn't curl like that in our village. I would award that very beautiful woman first prize for beauty in North, South and Central America. At the base of her neck we got a glimpse of cleavage . . . In our village not even a bare-naked woman would dare to wear such a plunging neckline. Her cleavage was opening the way Hell will open beneath our feet one day if we sin against Your commandments, God . . . That cleavage was offering us round, tempting apples . . . The apple trees around here can't produce apples to compare with them.

We men held our breath. We didn't need to breathe. Those who were smoking stopped inhaling. The smoke hung suspended in the air, motionless. It was as beautiful as the miracle of water changed into wine at the marriage at

Cana. As we looked, we wondered if we'd see anything so beautiful before the end of our lives. Then, once more, in a gust of wind, a snow flurry covered over the screen. The curtain of snow closed up again. The beautiful lady disappeared.

I had to think it all over, so I went outside. There, it was snowing as hard as on the television. I walked, hoping for another miracle, hoping the snow would open and an angel would appear to me.

Thank You, God, for giving us television.

5

Prayer for Becoming Good at Something

God, did Your father ever say to You: "Little God, you aren't good for anything?" Today, our father judged me. "You aren't good for anything!" he snarled. "I wonder if you'll ever make something of yourself in this world. You're fourteen years old, it's time you were useful. Those priests at the Petit Séminaire are turning you into a good-for-nothing. When I was your age, I was working like a man . . . You know what I was doing then. I've told you. I wasn't a good-for-nothing."

His story is as well known as the tune to "Au Clair de la lune." When he was my age, our father was ravaging the forests of Canada and the United States with his axe. I, his son, am translating into my French language the words of the greatest authors of Antiquity, because they wrote in idioms that normal people don't speak nowadays.

"You're a good-for-nothing!" our father said again. He didn't really mean that. He was trying to tell me something else. He didn't go to school for very long; he doesn't know all the ways you can speak or all the delicate nuances of our beautiful French language. He still hopes to make me Prime Minister of Canada. He wouldn't vote for a good-for-nothing in the election. On the other hand, our father was angry.

When he left for his business at the beginning of the week, he said to me: "Your summer holidays have started. Too much rest is bad for the health. A young man needs something to do with his hands to keep them out of his pockets. I want you to bring the wood into the cellar. Pile it into nice neat cords for me."

That was last Monday. I don't need to explain to You, God, that the wood is for heating the house during the winter. Our house is huge. It's exposed to the wind. Up here on the hill, the winters are long and cold. The wind is fierce and the fire demands an astronomical amount of wood.

Last Monday I found myself facing a Kilimanjaro, an Annapurna, an Everest of firewood I was supposed to move. It was the beginning of the week; my father wouldn't be back till Saturday, so I had a few days' grace. First of all, I thought. That's something I learned to do at the Petit Séminaire. It seemed to me that it should be possible to transform this mind-numbing chore into an exciting adventure. I'd read about how the Egyptians built the pyramids. I'd also read the history of the medieval cathedrals. With a little philosophy I'd get the best of this stupid woodpile.

I was still thinking about those great works of ancient times when Saturday landed on me. Along with Saturday came our father. The mountain of wood was just as he'd left it. He gazed at it for a moment, looking as if he'd just got a whiff of some stinky cheese. His silence was angry. I didn't know where to put my hands. They wanted to settle in my pockets, but my father

Prayer for
Becoming
Good at
Something

yells at me when I put my hands in my pockets. He delivered his decree as if he were spitting:

"You're a good-for-nothing!"

My father insulted me, he humiliated me, he disowned me, just because of a few pieces of wood . . . Right there, with him looking on, I stuffed my hands in my pockets. I didn't utter a single word. I took off down the gravel road that goes to the Quamme River. I felt like talking to You about it all, God, in private.

Am I a good-for-nothing? If our father is right, I'm going to close my books and let time flow over me like water over the back of a trout.

I'm not a good-for-nothing! Give me a mountain of books to read and I'll read them all without complaining, from the first page to the last. I don't have a natural gift for transporting logs. Our little brother would have fun doing that . . . Did You create me so I could pile up pieces of wood?

In his day, our father was forced to engage in that kind of mind-destroying work. Later on, he accepted the fact that I, his son, would undertake scholarly studies. Which meant that he didn't want his son to become a slave like him. Had he forgotten? My hands weren't made for splinters or blisters.

I'm not a bad son. I could do what he wants; I could fling those logs through the cellar window, pile them up from floor to ceiling in very tight rows as even as a brick wall; I could carefully cord them to ensure that the count was accurate and that the logger hadn't cheated us . . . But I don't feel like it.

According to my scientific calculations, a cord of wood contains on average five hundred and forty-four and a half logs. Because our father is sensitive to the cold, he buys thirty-three cords of wood every summer, or seventeen thousand, nine hundred and sixty-eight logs to throw through the cellar window, then pile and cord.

It isn't true that I'm a good-for-nothing. The books I read at the Petit Séminaire make my hands delicate, but I'm going to deal with that firewood. Next February when I'm in our dormitory at the Petit Séminaire, our family will have a well-stoked fire and a well-heated house. Quantities of smoke will pour from our chimney so that the fragrance of elm, birch and beech will mingle with the icy odour of the sky. God, it isn't true that I'm good for nothing.

I'll grant you that I'm not daring like the climber Maurice Herzog, who just conquered the summit of Annapurna. That's a mountain in the Himalayas and it stands twenty-six thousand, five hundred and sixty feet high. How do they calculate the height of a mountain? Why did You create us so ignorant, God? I wish I were daring like Maurice Herzog.

I'm not an ace like Babe Ruth, who hit fifty-nine home runs in 1921 and sixty in 1927. You who know everything must know that baseball player's name . . . I'm not a phenomenon like Maurice Richard, who drove the puck into the Toronto Maple Leafs' net five times on March 23, 1945. God, I'd like to hit the ball like Babe Ruth, I'd like to be a champion like Maurice Richard.

I'm not strong like the boxer Joe Louis, whose

birthday is May 13, like mine. And that's not all: the Brown Bomber won the heavyweight championship in 1937, the year I was born. Joe Louis lined up twenty-one victories by KO. Are You wondering what a KO is? What it means, God, is that after a KO his opponent looks like a bull coming out of the slaughterhouse. If I were a slugger like Joe Louis, I wouldn't have had a nosebleed during my fight on Good Friday, 1947, against Chou Racine, when he laid me out on the snow. God, I'd like to be strong like Joe Louis.

I'm not intrepid like Brick Bradford in the comics. Last week, Brick Bradford, at the controls of his Time Top, reached the centre of Earth. Another week, he explored the galaxy of atoms that move around in a one-cent coin. God, I wish I were intrepid like Brick Bradford.

I'm not a magician like Mandrake: he knows the magic word that will let him pass through a mirror and walk around on the other side, behind the reflections of things and people. God, I'd like to be a magician like Mandrake.

Have You heard of the great artist Prud'hon? He painted a woman who's so beautiful that I get dizzy when I look at her. She's fat, the lady. She's as white as milk. She is lying on a yellow veil. She has plump thighs. Her belly is like a balloon. Her right breast is as round as a scoop of ice cream and it's decorated with a nipple that looks like a cherry, but pointed. Prud'hon was born in 1758, one year before Quebec was invaded by the English. The lady's name is Psyche because the painting that shows her lying down is called *The Abduction of Psyche*. The young man who's abducting her is called Love. He's carrying the naked lady in his arms. I don't know why she's all naked. That beautiful woman was painted by the brilliant hand of a man. God, You didn't even give me enough talent to draw a tomato.

That holy picture slipped out of the Reverend Abbé Drouin's breviary during the Our Father when I was serving his mass. I picked it up. The Reverend Abbé Drouin whispered: "That's an angel." So I asked him: "Can I keep the picture for my prayers?"

I'll never be a great artist like Prud'hon. I'll never have a chance to carry a naked woman in my arms like Love. God, I'd like to be a great artist like Prud'hon.

I'm not a singer like Raoul Jobin, the tenor who makes the glasses ring in the cupboard when he strikes up "O Holy Night" on the radio. I'd like to sing Your praises too, God, but whenever I join in with the choir, the director turns his big ear in my direction and with his little hand that strokes the music as if it were a dog's head, he gestures to me to leave the group as fast as I can. I'd like to be a singer like Raoul Jobin.

I'm not an actor like Fred Ratté, the actor with a big nose. His sepulchral voice is scary. Sometimes it even makes the hair in old Ferdinand Chabot's wig stand on end. Fred Ratté is always surrounded by bursts of lightning, thunder growling, caves that open up like terrifying jaws, secret gates creaking with demonic laughter, coffins with lids that aren't properly sealed, big sabres dripping with blood . . . I won't tell You the rest . . .

A while ago, I'd have liked to act in a comedy by Molière. The Reverend Abbé Petit-Cheval turned me down . . . Instead he chose Symphorien Baguette, who has blond hair. I was very glad I'd been left out when I learned that the Reverend Abbé Petit-Cheval had given handsome Symphorien Baguette two bumps like the kind that grow on girls when the time comes. He put a blond wig on him too . . . And then a few days after that, handsome Symphorien Baguette was wearing a lace dress. The Reverend Abbé Petit-Cheval was bragging to everybody that Symphorien Baguette was more beautiful than a real girl. Symphorien Baguette wiggled and jiggled in his skirt and the Reverend Abbé Petit-Cheval was as flabbergasted as I'd been when I saw *The Abduction of Psyche*.

The great day for the show arrived. Parents came from the far-off countryside and even from town. The curtain opened. There stood Symphorien Baguette with his bumps, his wig, his low neckline and his cheeks covered with red make-up. When he opened his mouth to declaim Henriette's lines, we could hear the lowing of a bull that doesn't want to be taken to the slaughterhouse. His voice had changed that day. Molière had never been so funny . . . God, I'd like to be an actor like Fred Ratté.

I'm not brave like the thirteen men from our village who went to war to battle Hitler's soldiers. There was one who died. I wouldn't have liked to die like him, but I would have liked to liberate the scrawny children. They had shaved heads and sharp bones like on the poster in our father's store. I don't know how much Nazi game the soldiers from our village shot down . . . The ones who are still alive look fearless and blameless. The war has been over for a long time but they still parade in their uniforms. The one who died at the front can't parade with the others, but he was given a special funeral. The choir's singing was more off-key than usual. His coffin was carried by other soldiers who hadn't been killed. They also blew a trumpet at his burial. God, You made me be born too late to go to war. I'd like to be brave like the soldiers from our village.

I'm not quick like Superman. He can intercept a plane in the sky the way I can catch a baseball now and then. He could stack our father's wood in a fraction of a second, but it's not his strength that I envy. God, give me instead his ability to fly. I'd love to glide through the air like Superman! Like a meteor, I would fly over the great cities on Earth. I'd cross the sea. I'd see countries that can't be found. I would plunge into jungles. I would zigzag through space like a fish in water. I'd sit on the tops of the highest mountains. I'd discover waterfalls whose roaring no one else has heard. I would make my way around the Earth like the characters in *Pays et nations*, my set of illustrated books. I'd fly to the other planets in the Milky Way and even farther, God... I'll never be Superman. Why did You condemn me to wear out my soles in a cow pasture? God, I'd like to be as swift as Superman.

In the famous movie *Mr. Smith Goes to Washington*, Jimmy Stewart looks like a good-for-nothing, the way our father told me that I look. He looks like a lazy lump from Wisconsin. From the look of him, you can be sure that he'd post-pone stacking the wood in his father's cellar for as long as he could. Yet Jimmy Stewart gets elected to the American Senate. There, like an angry giant he attacks the pirates of politics. Those corrupt old politicians can't believe that they've been KO'd, laid out, by the big lazy lump from Wisconsin. Even after he became a great man, Jimmy Stewart still had the slightly wounded look of a man whose father has told him, "You're a good-for-nothing." God, I'd like to be just like Jimmy Stewart.

I'd also like to be a poet, God, like Émile Nelligan. During algebra classes, I'd like to string together verses like François Villon. His poems are so sad they still make you want to cry nearly six hundred years later. I'd like to copy the poet Rimbaud and travel to the ends of the earth, to the strange countries that resembled his dreams. I'd like to become a great poet, God.

I'm listening to the water in the Quamme River as it runs over the mossy stones. That music assures me that I'm good for something, even if I'm a little sad. The water tells me that our father knows I'm good for something too.

God, You've placed a dream inside me. It resembles the flame of a candle in a window that a person could walk towards if he were lost in the night.

Because of that dream, I'm not altogether happy. I always want to be somewhere else. In my skin, I feel like a caterpillar in its cocoon who wants to become a butterfly. Thank you, God, for placing that dream inside me.

If through Your holy will a nice fat trout were to take hold of my hook, I'm sure that our father would modify his verdict.

6

Prayer of the Little Soldier Who Stands at Attention

You are perfect, God, because You created women. There are days when I think You'd be even more perfect if You'd sent some to our Petit Séminaire for boys. All we think about is the women who aren't there.

You, who see everything, know that my little soldier is sticking out his chest, that he's standing up as proud as a rooster. He acts as if he's the Eiffel Tower in Paris. The little thing that used to dangle like a stringbean in the garden has become as proud as the Emperor Napoleon. When my little soldier stands at attention, I don't know how I should walk. It's as if I've grown a third leg. Is it a disease? Could it be a kind of tonsillitis down there below my belt?

In the refectory, there's Idola. She's the one who serves the soup. Her ladle, which is the size of a shovel, dips into a saucepan as deep as a barrel. Seen from behind, Idola has a bum like an elephant that's too wide to go through the circus gates. Seen from the front, Idola looks like a '51 Mercury with headlights that stick out way beyond the grille. The tips of her cones, as we say in geometry, go right through her apron. When I hold out my bowl to Idola behind her window, my little soldier thinks it's parade time. Is this caused by a germ?

I confessed my disease to my friend Long-Chapelet. He confided in me too: he's also caught the disease. And a number of similar cases have been noted in our class. Could it be an epidemic?

Yesterday, in their private domain, the big boys were telling dirty stories, like they usually do. I kept my distance from them, but I was listening. Curly Gonzague was showing a magazine that you can buy on Second Avenue but that's on the Index at the Petit Séminaire. It's a catalogue of girls who aren't wearing enough clothes for the rigorous winters we endure in these parts.

If I understood him correctly, a certain kind of Brazilian fish has a penis that breaks away like an independent fish to chase the female fish it has chosen. The big boys who are studying philosophy think that's hilarious. None of them believed Curly Gonzague's story. Did You really invent an animal like that, God? I'll have to study ichthyology too.

Ever since I heard that story I've been a little worried. Worried that men might work the way that Brazilian fish does. Could my little soldier break away and then go on a spree under the skirt of one of the girl students at the École des Infirmières du Pain Bénit? Please, God, don't let that happen. I don't want to become the father of a child whose mother had a son whose father no one knew the name of. What would happen if my penis mistook the black robe of one of Your priests for the real black dress of a widow in mourning? Please, God, don't let my mysterious little soldier get away from me. I need every little piece of the body that You gave me. On the other hand, I congratulate You for the two bumps You added to the girls. They do wonders for their appearance.

It isn't easy to confess all these things. I feel awkward, but I was anxious to talk to You about them. I'm preoccupied. I think a lot . . . This is all new. I don't understand. Our father has often said that at a certain point in his life, a man becomes as crazy as a calf that's leaving the stable to roll in the grass in the spring. I think that's what is happening to me. I don't sleep the way I used to. During the daytime I dream as if it were night. I feel restless. I'd like our Petit Séminaire to be filled with girls who come from the time when clothes weren't invented yet. I'm thirsty for girls. Why am I in a prison populated by boys? Down in the valley on the other side of the river, the École des Infirmières du Pain Bénit is crammed with girls. If You were able to separate the water of the Red Sea in two like an apple and build a road down the middle where Moses could walk without getting his sandals wet, You ought to be able to accomplish the miracle of combining the girls' school and our boys' school. With our little antennae sticking out we look like Martians trying to find out what we're doing here on Earth. Look at us, God!

The *Larousse* dictionary shows us beautiful goddesses who forgot to get dressed before they went out to have their portraits painted. It's understandable; they didn't need fur coats or long underwear in those sunny countries where winter doesn't exist. I can't conclude yet whether the women of Canada are built like those goddesses from Antiquity, but if they are, it must be pretty exciting to contemplate how they're built in the flesh. Just looking at Amphitrite, goddess of the oceans, seated on her sea serpent with her breasts exposed to the winds, on page 1075, my eyes are covered with mist, my brain spins in my head like a top, my heart leaps as if it were skipping rope; I have a pain in my stomach as if a cat were scratching me with all its claws, and my little soldier is standing like a baby bird on the edge of his nest who's spreading his wings for the plunge into infinity.

Since You're eternal, You must be pretty old. Your holy white beard has been growing for a long time. If You smoke a pipe like the old men, You probably reek of tobacco and your moustache must be brown like our uncle Eugène Fournier's. That's not very appealing. Young French Canadians pray to You, but the young Greeks and Romans must have been a lot more fervent than we are. I don't want to offend You, because You are the true God of the true religion, but I think it would be a lot easier to meditate before a beautiful naked goddess. I'm sure you'll agree that would be more enticing to pray to than an old beard that's turning yellow and stinks of a pipe . . . Please God, have pity on me!

On page 1742 of the dictionary we meet Venus, the goddess of love. Even though she's not totally naked, she's somebody you'd like to pray to! Her body is draped in a tunic with diaphanous folds. One of her breasts, the left one, is exposed like a beautiful bunch of grapes.

It's more interesting to look at one when you know that the other one's hidden. And all that's a lot nicer to look at than Your images, even when they're edged in gold.

Now, I know I have to pray to You, because You are the one and only true God, but I confess that I wouldn't have minded being a young Roman or Greek. For instance, at prayer-time, a boy my age could meditate before the goddess Fortune. Holding her horn of plenty, she stands balanced on a winged wheel. Her tunic is very short and nearly transparent. There's a blindfold over her eyes. I wonder why she hides her eyes instead of her behind. On page 1383, you can make out at least one and a third breasts. What a beautiful religion the Greeks and Romans had! Those goddesses make you want to go to Heaven. Was their religion really as false as we've been told?

Are You sure it was a good idea to replace their religion with Yours, even if Yours is the best because it's the only true one? You who created the entire world, the sea, the stars and everything we haven't yet discovered, You who can accomplish whatever wonders You want, convert those beautiful goddesses in my dictionary and bring them into Your holy religion. My friends and I would be a lot more pious!

Ever since my alert little soldier has been everready to go into battle, I'm often uneasy. I'd much rather he stayed peacefully asleep the way he used to. It's embarrassing. The other day we had a violin recital. The parents were invited to the Petit Séminaire, including the mothers and sisters. Even the girls from the École des Infirmières du Pain Bénit were there. Never in history had so many curly heads been seen at the Petit Séminaire. It was the first time since the Flood that there were girls inside our paddock. It was the first time the rustle of girls' skirts was heard in our building. Accustomed to the strict shuddering of black soutanes stained with soup and smelling of tobacco and incense, the corridors were jumping for joy at the aroma of backsides washed with scented soap. Never had girls' behinds sat on our chairs, which were crackling with excitement.

Our mother was proud. I'd been chosen to read the violinist's introduction. I was waiting in the wings. The artist was wearing a dress that hadn't been approved of by the bishop. It was very long at the bottom but very short at the top. Its low-cut neckline showed her shoulders and even the glimmer of her apples. Did she think she was a Greek goddess? I gazed at the landscape and thought: "If she bends over even a little, I'll be able to see her musical belly-button!"

When it was time to step on to the stage, my little soldier stood up when I did. If You'd been in my place, God, would you have known how to walk? My head was spinning. Was it the effect of the perfume of the girls from the École des Infirmières du Pain Bénit? I think my little soldier would have liked to introduce the violinist himself. The only thing there was to shelter me was the microphone cord. I positioned myself carefully behind it but, as Aristotle said, a cord is only a cord.

Do nighttime dreams mean something? Are they messages that You send at night because humans are too distracted in the daytime? Are they a liberty the soul doesn't dare to take in the daylight? I'd really like to know. If I knew, maybe I could understand the dream I dreamed last night that I came here, to Your chapel, to tell You.

In my dream, it was morning. I was about to shave my beard as I do every two weeks. I was surprised when I saw in the mirror not my face, but my little soldier. I wasn't there. There was just my little soldier. I put away the razor. And then my little soldier got dressed in my clothes; he tied my tie and slipped on my shoes and then he went to morning mass with the other students. No one noticed that he was there. My little soldier sang the hymns in Gregorian chant. Later, he went to class and handed in his translation of a paragraph from *De viris illustribus*. When classes were over, my little soldier played in my position on our basketball team. He pitched the ball from very far away and it slipped right into the net. That was when I woke up. God, could You explain to me why You inflict such nightmares on a well-behaved boy?

In any case, God, when I start chasing girls and being horny like the big boys, I wonder what I'll do with my little soldier that's so often in the way. That's a problem You don't have, God, because You're invisible.

Could you give my little soldier some of Your invisibility?

69

Prayer of the
Little Soldier
Who Stands
at Attention

7

Prayer for the
Shovelful of Gravel

I've just read in a book, God, that You don't exist. Before speaking out so categorically the author should have observed the ants in his garden and the stars in the sky. How could they have been created without You? The great thinker ought to know that even an ordinary maple syrup pie can't bake itself.

Before I went to bed tonight, I looked up at Your sky. Now, in July, it's so transparent a person can practically see You in Your dwelling place, behind that curtain of blue silk. I gazed for a long time at Your firmament. I did something very bad today. If You are assessing the inhabitants of Earth tonight, You mustn't be very proud of this little guy with the aching biceps and the blisters on his hands who made very bad use of the intelligence that You inserted into his skull. My intelligence isn't the most powerful in the world yet, but it's the reason why my French-Canadian Catholic family sent me away to study books. My classmates left to work in factories and the forest.

My intelligence understands the difficult grammar of the French language. It allowed me to learn Latin like the young Romans of ancient times, and Greek like the young Athenians. It also lets me absorb algebra. I don't know yet what good all that will do me, but I thank You for giving me a normal amount of intelligence. You gave Boniface Ledoux only a quarter of an ounce. He's fourteen like me, but You put a potato under his hair instead of a brain.

Yet tonight I've got tears in my eyes. With his potato that will never learn Latin or Greek or the subtleties of the French language or the excitement of algebra, Boniface Ledoux is a better person than I am. Though I've been given the gift of a fine intelligence, I was wicked. God, does more intelligence make humans more wicked?

At the school in the village, Boniface Ledoux was at least five years behind the worst of the bad pupils. But he never harmed a soul, even though we always laughed at him. When we wanted to have some fun we'd punch him. He didn't punch back. That game was an invention of our normal intelligence. Does intelligence make us wicked? In any case, it does make us pretentious.

In our villages on the hills, the air is good, the children are ruddy-cheeked and strong. At fourteen, we don't have delicate little arms like the girls. It's time to start working like men. Today, I started to work like a man. I've got so many blisters on my hands it was hard to hold my soup spoon. My back is as sore as if my bones were broken. If I move under my sheet, it hurts. Yet I didn't work as hard as Boniface Ledoux. He's a lot less intelligent than I am, but he's as tough as a grown man. You gave him the intelligence of a sparrow, but the strength of a draught horse.

For a long time we used to envy men who

worked. We couldn't wait until we were part of the group of men who do something with their arms. Those who were chosen, like me, to study all the things you have to know in order to guide our French-Canadian people along the road of its destiny, we were even more eager to work than men who'd never studied.

I was as proud as a king this morning at a quarter after six. The new sunbeams were shattering in the dew and on the daisies. We drove through the village in the dump truck along with Boniface Ledoux and some old men like Boozy Gédéon and Cursewords Lapierre. Monsieur Labranche, who's head of the municipal roadworks, was driving. We were part of the team the government had hired to repair the roads. The government wanted to make the voters happy before the election. When the government calls an election, it needs people like us.

I was so glad to be working with my hands at last. After the translations of ancient texts, the sermons that go on for two hours, the prayers we have to keep saying over and over, after the history classes that recount the woes of our French-Canadian people who are walking under the dark clouds of the future, after nights spent wondering if I ought to become the Prime Minister of Canada or a great poet like Ronsard, that old fellow who loved young girls and wrote them love letters, after all the time I'd spent at the Petit Séminaire, I was glad to be in the back of that truck. In the light of Your sun, God, that was as radiant as Your wisdom, we were on our way to the gravel quarry.

My work boots were new. The leather shone. My overalls were new. My shovel gleamed like a dessert spoon. It was the first day of my life as a grown man. The future was coming to me. A member of the French-Canadian élite, I stood proud and unashamed among the workers. I would not betray the humblest among them— the drawers of water, the ploughmen of the soil, the shovellers of gravel. Into one back pocket I'd slipped an American novel and into the other a small English dictionary where I can't find all the words in the novel.

You saw how eagerly I thrust my shovel into the gravel, how fervently I flung my first shovelful into the truck! Of course, one shovelful of gravel in a truck is like a pinch of salt in the sea. That's what I told myself after twenty shovelfuls. The bones in my skeleton were being dislocated, the muscles were knotting in my back. My hands on the handle of my shovel were burning as if I were holding a red-hot poker. The others were smoking and shovelling gravel with movements that were slow, regular, nearly subdued. They were flinging gravel the way I turn the pages of a dictionary. Shovelling gravel seemed to be as easy for them as smoking. Boniface Ledoux was more assiduous than the others. He'd throw three shovelfuls while the others were satisfied with one. He smoked faster than the others, too. He's my age and he smokes a pipe . . . Our father also smoked a pipe when he was the age of Boniface Ledoux. The first time I dared to smoke a cigarette, our mother went to see her own mother, our grandmother; she cried as if I'd committed a crime that deserved the gallows. Boniface

Ledoux's mother doesn't stop him from smoking. Maybe she hopes the tobacco will give him a little intelligence. Boozy Gédéon and Curse-words Lapierre, not drinking, not cursing, were peacefully performing their task like two fine oxen pulling a cart. While I was thinking that I was like a butterfly who was struggling to carry a stone. I plugged away. My strength was depleted. I was working myself to death. To become a man it isn't enough to study books; I knew that, I'd heard it from our father's mouth often enough: the only school for learning about life is work.

Monsieur Labranche, the boss of the municipal roadworks, had his hands in his pockets as he admired the fields. Lapierre yelled at him, with a stream of curses I won't repeat to You:

"It wouldn't hurt your health to do a little work, Labranche!"

The boss replied:

"My job is thinking. I'm the boss and the boss has to think for the rest of you. In the grand scheme of things, it's more exhausting to think than to shovel."

One day I'll be a boss and I'll do a lot of thinking. While waiting for that moment, I continued transferring gravel to the truck. I was exhausted. My arms refused to bend. I could barely lift my empty shovel. So then I did what I'll do when I'm a boss. I started to think. I even asked You for a little of Your strength, God, so I could finish my day's work. Beside me, Boniface Ledoux kept working away as if he intended to come out on the other side of the Earth, down under, in Australia. He didn't even look tired.

Finally, the truck was full. Monsieur Labranche broke off his reflection and started the truck. We were relieved to see it disappear. We wouldn't have to lift a single shovelful till it came back! Boniface Ledoux was watching the truck climb the hill with a certain sadness. He'd have preferred not to be obliged to stop shovelling. I was out of breath, with scalding pains in my back, my shoulders and my arms. Under its load of gravel, the truck, clattering through the spruce trees, resembled a hard-working old elephant.

Half an hour later, Monsieur Labranche came back. Right off the bat, he announced:

"I have to go into the woods. I've got too many responsibilities. I'm tense. I need some peace and quiet so I can think. I'm the boss. My job is to think. I'm the head. The rest of you are the arms. So I think—and you shovel."

And he left us.

We went back to work. One after the other, each of us lifted his shovelful. Boniface Ledoux had had time to pitch three. The gravel was as heavy as iron. We all stopped, except for Boniface Ledoux. Cursewords Lapierre blamed You, God, for inventing work. Boozy Gédéon kept eyeing the flask we'd seen him hide in the grass, in the shadow of a big rock. He went over to Boniface.

"Boniface," he suggested, "I'd be prepared to bet a good pipeful of strong *canadien* tobacco you can't fill the truck on your own."

That big child to whom You gave only a pinch of intelligence, God, grunted:

"Boniface not need help. Boniface fill truck all alone. Boniface want tobacco."

He went to work on that gravel as if it were music. Stones and lumps went flying towards the truck. At that rate, Boniface Ledoux seemed strong enough to shovel the entire world.

Cursewords Lapierre stretched out in the grass. Ecstatic, he started bombarding Your sky with oaths. He was only trying to tell You in his own way how beautiful Your nature was to him. Boozy Gédéon pulled his flask out from behind its stone to quench his thirst and start him on a lengthy glide towards bliss.

While I . . . God, You gave me more intelligence than You gave Boniface Ledoux; yet I sat down, I leaned my back against one of those big spruce trees that grow in rocky soil, and there, in the scented shadows, I read *The Catcher in the Rye*, looking up the words in my little dictionary.

Meanwhile, Boniface Ledoux was working like a slave. It's because I've been thinking about it that here in my bed tonight, I'm crying.

8

Prayer about Eating Lunch with a Great Man

Today, I ate at the same table as a legislative councillor. He was sitting right across from me, in the flesh. Even though he'd sprinkled himself with cologne, I could smell the tobacco on his suit. He was so close that when he sneezed, I got sprayed. I wiped it off, quickly but politely. I never would have thought that one day I'd be so close to a great man. The legislative councillor was eating with me and I was eating with him, on the same tablecloth. Thank You, God, for delegating a great man to appear along my road.

Before he turned up, I was all alone at my table at the back of the dining room. I'd prefer a table elsewhere, near the window, so I could admire the lake and the girls on the beach in bikinis, but the headwaiter always urges me to sit at that one near the washrooms. When he first saw me, his little rat-tail moustache got excited and he pinched his nose as if I stank. My red-and-black-checked shirt, my overalls and my workboots spoiled his fancy dining room decorated with artificial flowers that he's probably stupid enough to water. A shoveller of gravel: I'm dressed for shovelling gravel. And if the headwaiter thinks I'm not fancy enough, that's tough. I am building a road for the future of our people.

Eat somewhere else? I'd love to. Unfortunately, the local MP is also the owner of the hotel. And the local MP is the man who told our father that there was a job in gravel for me. Because I'm growing too fast and because the work is hard, he recommended to our father that, for my health, I take my meals in his hotel. Under our good government, roadworks and the hotel business go hand in hand.

According to our father, this is the best government in French-Canadian history. It is protecting us from atheistic Communism, Your mortal enemy. Hurray for our government!

However, because of goddamn politics, I'm condemned to eat my meals next to the washrooms. And there's so much coming and going . . .

The buses also belong to the local MP. At meal time, tourists stop at the hotel. I'm not making this up.

Even the legislative councillor couldn't get a table by the window with a view of the girls. The only chair available was the one at my table. I recognized the great man right away. Every week, his photograph appears in the regional newspaper. Every week, the caption under his photo recounts the senator's words and deeds. "Last Thursday, our beloved legislative councillor attended the funeral of the late lamented Théophile Labonté, notary and friend of our good government." The following week, we read: "Our valiant legislative councillor was observed at the marriage of Léopoldine Lafleur, homemaker, and Félicien Deschamps, handyman, who will no doubt provide our good government with a number of little voters." Fairly often we read under his photo: "Here is our distinguished legislative councillor, whose eldest son, world-famous in the field of music, will present a concert this week, assisted by his wife, who also plays music, in the beautiful city of Quebec."

I'd never have thought that such a famous man would sit down with a mere student. But yes, he did sit down—with me! Out of politeness, I closed my book, *The Catcher in the Rye*, which I would have liked to keep open. I'd got to the part where Holden Caulfield . . . But there's no need to describe it to You, God. It's not Your kind of book. Besides, it's in English, and I'm sure You prefer your literature in French.

To impress me, the legislative councillor tried to make eye contact. Now, You know that I'm big for my age, thin and rather lanky. When people look at me, my cheeks flush and burn.

"Little student, do you know who's come to sit at the same table as you, as if you were somebody important?"

I looked up, but instead of going towards the great man, my eyes came to rest on the bathroom doorknob. Never in my life had I been so close to a famous man. I didn't dare look at him. The only famous great men I'd ever associated with were those in my schoolbooks, and they'd been dead for a long time.

"Little student, not everyone is lucky enough to sit with a legislative councillor. You'll remember this day for the rest of your life. I am the father of a very fine French-Canadian, Roman Catholic, prolific family. Our brave ancestors came to Canada from Poitou in the year of our Lord 1619. My eldest son has inherited my musical talent. He's a world-renowned artist. The whole of our beautiful city of Quebec knows him. My other son has inherited my gift for politics. I've got thirteen good and attractive children. Every one of them has inherited one of my talents. I've even passed some of them on to my daughters. Besides that, they're lovely plump girls. I enjoy the close friendship of the Premier of the Province of Quebec. When he and I go fishing, there's no one else he trusts to dig his worms. I know every one of the ministers in our good government. They always invite me to the christening of their newborns. I'm on first-name terms with those honourable gentlemen. I'm the godfather of sixty-seven children in all parts of the Province of Quebec. I know all the Members of Parliament. I also know the Opposition members, even though I'm absolutely opposed to the idea that we need an Opposition. My opinion is based on the following sound, logical reasoning: the Province of Quebec is governed by a good government. Why then do we need an Opposition that's always trying to harm the good government? Nowhere in all of Canada is there a greater democrat than me. But I'm telling you, young man, the Opposition is a waste of public funds. Being a democrat doesn't mean throwing away the public funds of the poor people."

While he was airing his opinions, I had meticulously prepared what I would say:

"I'm delighted to meet a legislative councillor, Monsieur."

"You've been hired by the road department. I know that. Our party is interested in good students who will become good politicians. Politics is the lifeline of our people. Now, I've noticed that you're reading a book in English. That's a good thing to do, learn English. English is the language of business, just as Latin is the language of prayer. French Canadians have just one flaw: they know too much Latin and not enough English. Take your example, little student. You've learned more Latin than English. And where are you today? Today, you're standing on a pile of gravel like poor old Job on his dung heap."

Was that an insult? I decided that I'd defend myself:

"I won't spend my whole life shovelling gravel..."

"Job on his dung heap knew a lot more Latin than you ... Now me, I've forgotten the very notion of what poverty is. A lot of people think I'm a millionaire. They're all wrong. I am more than a millionaire. To remind myself about poverty, now and then I go and look at a poor man. Today, little student, I'm seeing you..."

Was that another insult? God, I felt like leaving my table. But, well, one of the desserts on the menu was maple syrup pie with ice cream . . .

"Are you listening? Look at me. Can you look a legislative councillor in the eye when he's speaking to you? Are you too embarrassed?"

I could feel my face turn as red as a strawberry pie. My head stayed bowed. My eyes avoided the senator's face.

"Little student, if you can't look a legislative councillor in the eye, will you be able to look at the future? Timidity is the blessed affliction of the French-Canadian people. Are we preparing yet another generation that will blush and lower their eyes like virgins who're still virgins? By the Blessed Virgin, is the French-Canadian people going to go on wallowing in its misery? Our people need leaders who look the future squarely in the eye . . . Now listen carefully, little student . . . At your Petit Séminaire, do you study Aristotle?"

"Yes."

"Do you also study Plato, Socrates, Virgil,

Caesar, Homer, Molière and even Shakespeare?"

"Yes."

"Those great geniuses lived in the past; they teach you wisdom for the past."

"Yes."

"Little student, I'm going to teach you wisdom for the future . . . First of all, you're going to drink a glass of wine."

He filled my glass right to the rim. He clinked his glass against mine and then drained it in one gulp. I drank as quickly as I could. The legislative councillor didn't choke. Again he filled our glasses and we drained them.

"Look at me."

I tried to obey, but I couldn't. My pupils were covered with fog, my eyelids were closing. I didn't need a mirror to know that my face was redder than my shirt.

"By the Blessed Virgin, I don't want to meet any more young French Canadians who're as timid as a young nun who hasn't grown a beard yet. Now listen carefully, little student. After I've taught you what I'm going to teach you,

you'll be cured of your embarrassment. You'll be cured of your sickness. You'll be able to look whoever you want in the eye. Now then, let's raise our glasses and drink!"

This time, I didn't choke.

"You're intimidated by me. I can understand that. I am an impressive individual. Despite my modest manner, I'm a great man. My friends are great men. I'm important all over the Province of Quebec. It's perfectly normal that you should be intimidated by me. Now I'm going to tell you a secret. A secret that the priests at your Petit Séminaire have never dared to teach you. Listen carefully, young student: after he's relieved his bowels, every man turns around to examine his turd. I myself am an honourable member of the Legislative Council and every morning, I turn around to look closely at my turd . . . Now then, little student, you're going to look me right in the eye and you're going to repeat to yourself: 'The Honourable Legislative Councillor salutes his turd every morning.'"

First, I silently pronounced the words of the

powerful man. Then I delivered them aloud. Were they magic words? My face didn't feel at all red. We drank another glass of wine.

"I always take the time to turn around and salute my turd. I can assure you that all the legislative councillors do the same. All the cabinet ministers do it, all the MPs. The Opposition members actually do it twice, because it takes them longer to understand. The Premier turns around to see his turd. His Majesty Louis XIV did it. Even the Pope in Rome, who is infallible, does it. It's a universal principle. You find it in Rabelais, in Molière . . . Young student, remember the principle: you can't be intimidated by a man when you know that he turns around to bid his turd farewell before he parts with it. That may be the most important principle you'll ever hear. And I've taught it to you because, by the Blessed Virgin, I don't want to see a single French Canadian intimidated by someone."

We drank another glass of wine.

"Try again, little student," he ordered. "Look me right in the eyes without blushing."

I pictured the great man with his pants down, bending over his natural production and giving his turd a friendly wave before it left on its journey. And then I locked eyes firmly with him. Not a hint of redness in my face. I was cured.

"Hallelujah!" he exclaimed. "Bring me another bottle!"

I still have a headache as I'm praying to You, God, but the legislative councillor freed me from my shyness. Thank You for putting him along my path.

Will the people whom I'm going to meet know my secret? If I knew that while they were looking at me, they were thinking that I turn around to wave goodbye to my turd, I'd be shy all over again.

9

Prayer of Someone
Who Would Like
to Know Where
He Comes From

I am fifteen years old, I've read a number of books, and I've done a great deal of thinking. I no longer believe everything that I used to believe. I'm older now. God, I'm questioning Your existence. Some very famous philosophers have done the same thing. If I stop believing in You, I won't pray to You any more. You won't hear my voice any more. Then You'll feel the way I do, since I never hear Yours.

Today, I'd like to address a little prayer to You, one that's packed full of questions. Here in this world where You've planted me, I'm attacked on all sides by questions. Important questions. I've even read them on a picture by Gauguin, a French painter who lived on an exotic island where there were beautiful girls. And I found a book in the library whose title is the same as my question: *Where Do We Come From?*

Can You answer that question, God? I need to know. And don't tell me: "I have always been, I am eternal." That doesn't explain anything. Who are the father and mother of eternity? Who gave You the gift of eternity? Do You understand me?

Unfortunately, asking that question is a sin. Our Catholic religion teaches us that You are the only God, the only beginning, the only end. Do You think I'm any further ahead with that?

As You can see, I'm thinking. You provided me with intelligence and I'm trying to use it. Why should I have to guess where I come from? That's complicated. It would be a lot simpler if You just told us the story in detail. It's no fun to land on earth without knowing where you've come from. Do You hide the truth from us? Where do I come from?

My teachers assure me that You have always

been. But they weren't there to check. They are here today, but not one of them could write in his report that he'd spotted You at the corner of the street.

We've arrived at the year 1952, and in the entire history of the world no one has ever taken Your picture. I'll probably never see You in my lifetime. If you are perfect, why do You hide yourself like a bandit who's being sought by the American FBI?

In life there is always something *before* something else, and there's always someone *before* someone else. Let me explain. Before the fine weather, there is rain. Before spring, winter. Before the flower, the seed. Before the son, the father. Before day, there is night. Before the beam, the tree. Before the chick, the egg, and before the egg, there's the hen. Before old age, there is youth. What was there *before* You, God?

I have a lot of respect for Your perfection, but still I dare to ask: Do You know the answer to my question? Excuse me, but Your boy is tired of not knowing.

I've learned how parents make children. Those magic tricks don't sound like very much fun. What I'm interested in is what the *before* was really like. *Before* everything began, when there was *nothing*. How did that *nothing* begin? How did that *nothing* give birth to *everything* that exists? If I had an answer to these questions I could gaze at Your sky the way a child gazes at his family's house. I'd stop looking like an idiot who's forgotten the most important thing in the world. Where does our Earth come from? In a book they explain that it's a small scrap that came loose from the Sun. So where did the Sun spring from?

Father Légaré, the English teacher, told us about a very old poet who wrote before English became the English that the English can understand. That poet was also a monk. In one poem, he compared life to a bird. He tells about how the bird is flying through a night that's as dense as dark blue ink. Suddenly, in the distance, he spies a spark. The bird is attracted to that point of light. As he draws closer the light grows. It is the vast window of a castle. It's wide open to the breeze. The bird discovers a huge room lit by thousands of candles. A party is going on there. The guests are eating, drinking, dancing. Mingled with the music are laughter, cries, the words of tales and discussions. The bird flies through the party. At the other end of the room, another window is open, all blue, nearly black, onto the night outside. Just as he was drawn by the light, the bird is now attracted by the night. He flies outside and continues flying through the dense darkness. And that, according to the old monk who was also a poet, is life.

97

Prayer of
Someone
Who Would
Like to Know
Where He
Comes From

God, I'd like You to tell me: Who built the castle? What was there *before* the night that enveloped the castle? What was there *before* the bird?

Our Earth resembles a rowboat filled with shipwreck victims who don't remember what port they sailed from. Pushed by the waves, they don't know towards what shore they are drifting. From what *Titanic* in distress has our small craft fallen away, God?

I know what it says in Your Bible: "God said: 'Let there be light' and there was light." Between You and me, I'm sure the real story's not so simple. As our father says, everything in life is complicated, even the things that aren't... Where did the candle come from that You lit, God? If You pressed a switch, who screwed in the bulb?

Apparently You separated the land from the seas. Where did the seas come from? Where did the land come from?

Why did You decide to create the world when You did? And when exactly did You do it? No one knows the date of Creation. Yet it's much more important than the date when America was discovered, in 1492. All the pupils in our class have known that date for ages, even our history teacher who claims that America was discovered long before Columbus by the Indians themselves on some unknown date...

Why did You stop creating? The Creation of the world isn't finished. Why are You no longer creating nowadays? Why didn't You decide today to command: "Let there be a ladder to the Moon!"? Immediately a fine new wooden ladder would appear and I'd start climbing up it to the Moon. During the worldwide massacre of war, why didn't You say: "Let there be peace on earth"? When the atomic bomb was dropped on Japan, why didn't You order: "Become a shower of roses on Hiroshima"? It would have obeyed You. Why aren't You brave enough to say: "Let death disappear"?

The Creation of the world is something from bygone days. You, God, are like a National Hockey League champion who scored all his goals four thousand generations ago. I don't understand: You showed imagination over six days in those far-off times; on the seventh day You decided to take Your nap. Have You woken up from it, God? Or are You still asleep? Modern times are here.

Voltaire, the great French philosopher, compared the Universe to a clock. He was sure that a clock is incapable of manufacturing itself and assembling its parts. According to him, a clock needs a clockmaker. That reasoning seems a little feeble to me. First of all, what proof is there that the Universe can be compared with a clock? And anyway, it's not because there's a clockmaker that a clock appears . . . And if the Universe was built by a clockmaker, who were the clockmaker's mother and father? Who were his grandfather and grandmother? Why did that eternal clockmaker create a clock that's not eternal? According to the prophets, at the end of the world that clock will disintegrate into a rabbit fart!

Apparently some scholars are convinced that everything that exists is the result of chance. Have You ever seen a strawberry pie sprinkled with powdered sugar that was baked by chance? I wish those people would explain to me where chance comes from. Is it the son of chance, the way I'm the son of our father? I'd like to know who the grandfather of chance was, and even his ancestor. What was there *before* chance? If there was nothing, what chance met all the conditions so that, by chance, there was nothing?

Through what chance was that nothing created? What was there *before* that nothing? I'm not Aristotle but I'm quite sure that the world didn't light on reality by chance, like a fly on the tip of Your divine nose.

A world created in six days! That's a beautiful story . . . but I've studied a little geology, a little chemistry, a little mineralogy, a little astronomy. Those sciences ask questions that You never answer. "In the beginning there was chaos," says the Bible. All I want to know, God, is what was there *before* chaos in order to build chaos? Create the world in six days . . . Isn't that a little boastful? "Let there be light!" The Universe is vaster than our dormitory where porky Père Lépine switches on the light at twenty to six every morning. Flooding the Universe with light must take time, even if light travels at the speed of light. It took humans centuries to invent shoelaces. I'm sure light wasn't invented at the flick of a finger . . . Or cows, or trout, or stones, or bees, or mothers . . . To have had the idea of creating light, You would have had to be tired of the night. Who are the father and mother of night? What was there *before* the night? It's at night that the light is beautiful. It was a poet who expressed that rather dull idea... The more I try to understand, the deeper I sink into lack of comprehension.

Some who don't believe in Your Bible claim that man is descended from monkeys, and woman too. Were Adam and Eve a monkey and his mate who'd escaped from a zoo that can't be found today? Is the idea of Eden simply a happy memory that humans have retained from the time when, wearing their monkey costumes, they were happy among the mangroves and the other jungle trees? Where did those monkeys come from? Where did the fleas in the monkeys' coats come from? Where do we come from, God? Why are You holding on to the answer to that question as if it were a state secret? Children who don't get answers to their questions invent their own.

In the United States a learned man claims that the Universe was created when one atom exploded! When I was eight years old, atoms burst over Japan. It was the biggest bang in the history of the world, yet no one saw a pair of new monkeys emerge from that explosion! After that big bang no one saw fields of stars, or troops of horses, or constellations of planets, or ocean depths crammed with whales and salmon, or groups of girls cut like diamonds, or gardens of flowers, or populations of snakes.

I want that learned man to tell me: *Before*, at the beginning, who produced the first atom that blew up? Who caused the explosion? To whom did the ears belong that heard the Big Bang? If no one heard it, some philosophers would conclude that there was no Big Bang. Did You hear the detonation, God? As far as I know, You didn't talk about it in Your Bible.

Where do we come from? Who are we? Are we "poor humans," as the poet Villon wrote, insects? Debris from fallen stars? Ferocious animals? Angels without wings? Flowers that can move? Were we modelled from dust that fell from the planets? Are we pieces of time? Are we the sparks of days already past? Are we fragments of ideas, scraps of anxiety, wisps of straw that have drifted down from paradise? Are we bees without wings, butterflies without colours? Are we fugitives from another world, immigrants to this planet?

As the painter Gauguin asked, Who are we, God? Where do we come from, where are we going?

While I'm praying to You now, God, I'm looking at the sky. It resembles a great open book. God, You haven't finished writing all the answers to our questions.

While I'm waiting to understand, I'll go and play basketball.

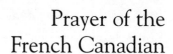

10

Prayer of the French Canadian

I thank You, God, for creating me a French Canadian, because our French-Canadian grandmother sings old songs from France. She wrote me a letter. I didn't think she knew how to write. In her letter I spotted a few old words, the kind you see in books by writers who died before the city of Quebec was founded in 1608. She also sent me a little money, warning me: "Don't go buying books with this humble offering. Learn how to waste a little on the sweet things in life. It's important for life to taste good."

Thank You for giving me a French-Canadian grandfather. When I was little he'd have me climb up on an old chair that had its paint worn off so that my little arms could help his strong arm to work the big leather bellows that blew on the fire crackling in his forge. On nights when there was no wind, at sunset he'd perform a touching ceremony. The farmers would come from far away so he could fix the wheels of their horse-drawn wagons. He'd begin by resting on bricks on the ground the iron rim that surrounded the wooden wheels. Then he'd arrange wedges of dried maple that crossed all around the circumference. After that, he'd sprinkle them with gasoline, as solemnly as Your priest sprinkling holy water. Finally, he'd pass me the burning match so I could drop it onto the best spot. In the dusk, the flames would briskly draw a little constellation that ended up here on Earth. The sparks would fly away like comets. Our grandfather would supervise the magic. At the right moment, his big tongs would grasp the red-hot hoop to tighten it around the wooden rim like a blazing necklace. Our French-Canadian grandfather was showing me a very ancient ritual. During the winter, while he was waiting for Your sun, Your flowers and Your mosquitoes, our grandfather worked with wood. He taught me the names of the different varieties and how to tell their perfumes apart. In his shop that was warmed by the smoke from his pipe, I didn't say anything, but I thought about all the wonders there are to discover in life. Please God, don't let me forget what he taught me.

He also showed me how to sharpen a hand-saw. There are times when what I read in my books seems as frivolous as soap bubbles. But then I remember that I know how to strike red-hot iron on the anvil and how to saw wood. And I tell myself that the thinkers who wrote those books should have had a grandfather like ours.

You gave us a second French-Canadian grandfather too, our father's father. He's always talking about people who are dead today who were alive in the olden days, as if the present time didn't exist. He has as many memories as if he were a thousand years old, as a poet on the Index says. Under the drooping branches of the great willows outside his house, his own grand-father had set up a game of croquet. That's a boring game. Luckily, the hens came there to peck. Our mallets would drive the ball in their direction and the birds would take off, flapping their wings. They thought they'd laid a big round egg that was chasing them.

Also, sitting on stakes on the lawn, there are airplanes carved from cedar. When the wind comes up, their propellers turn with a happy sound that I'll remember till I'm fifty and even older, if I live that long. Thank You, God, for giving me a French-Canadian grandfather who carved those propellers and wings with his pocketknife.

Our grandfather assures me that there's as much gold in the stream at the end of his land as there is in the Yukon. When we go there to dip our toes, we're careful not to disturb the nuggets. He tells us: "I've never touched that gold because a man commits a terrible sin when he gets rich. But if the great depression ever comes back, I'll go to that stream. I'll just bend down and I'll pick up a handful of gold that the good Lord was good enough to give to His Christians, just like He hands out horse buns to His sparrows." After we'd listened to our father's father, we knew that misery could never catch us; we felt safe on the earth. Now that I'm fifteen I've stopped believing in our paternal grandfather's gold.

Our paternal French-Canadian great-grandfather I never saw alive. His photograph hangs in our grandparents' bedroom, between the black crucifix and the blue Blessed Virgin. The great-grandfather has a thick moustache under his nose. You're going to say that's the best place for a moustache, and You'll be right. I'll soon have a beard myself. I'm going to hide my big nose in a moustache as luxuriant as our ancestor's. I'll also have my picture taken for my descendants, who'll thank You for providing them with a great-grandfather who sported a fine moustache.

Everyone I know is protected by two grandmothers. Our family has three. Our friends don't believe us. Thank You, God, for our third grandmother. You came and took our father's first wife and replaced her with a second one, who became our mother when I was born. I didn't know our father's first wife.

Once a year, on Saint-Jean Baptiste Day, we go to visit our third grandmother, the mother of our father's first wife. As soon as she sees us, she offers us little maple sugar animals that she's moulded for us. She's old, but she doesn't complain.

"Take a good look at me, youngsters, I'm not a scrawny little thing like my daughter who let herself die. At the age I am now, I should've been six feet under long ago . . . When you're French Canadian, you've got a strong heart and you mustn't let yourself die."

Thank You God for our French-Canadian ancestors. I don't know them because the history books don't talk about the ones who didn't kill any Indians or English. Our ancestors left their land of France to come to Canada three hundred years ago. After they'd disembarked from their ships, they defended themselves against blizzards and ice, they drove back the forest with their axes, they cut stone to erect churches for You, they squared off pine trees to build houses for themselves. If they passed on their strength to their descendants, God, I'll be able to make my way, sturdy and confident, along the road of our country's future.

You had me be born to a French-Canadian mother, and I thank You for that. Before she became our mother, to get used to children she was a teacher in the poor wooden school that leans up against the forest at the bottom of the hill. The planks of the wall let in the icy, wheezing north winds of winter. If the people in that part of our parish know how to read the newspaper, if they can write letters to complain to the government, and if they're able to rhyme off the date when Canada was discovered, that of the founding of the city of Quebec, and even that of the defeat at the Plains of Abraham, it's thanks to our mother. They should be grateful to her for having taught them that in our French language, the plural of the word *pou* takes an *x*, not an *s*. If it weren't for her, they'd have had no idea about that.

Now our mother's former pupils have wrinkles, grey hair and children, like her. When they talk about the old school that crackled in the cold and the old stove that didn't give off enough heat to thaw their fingers as they held their pens, they sound as if they loved those years, and they'd like to go back there with our mother as their teacher. As she listens to them, she seems prepared to explain God's Ten Commandments and the Seven Deadly Sins to them.

It was our mother who decided to send me away to study at the Petit Séminaire, where it isn't cold. A lot of books were waiting in the library for me to read, even some that were forbidden by Your Pope and Your bishops. My friend Long-Chapelet and I managed to take a few books from the inferno of not being read they'd been condemned to. God, Your church doesn't seem to like French literature very much. Thank You, God, for giving me a French-Canadian mother who keeps a big blue-covered notebook in her drawer, in which she's copied out her favourite poems.

You also entrusted me to a French-Canadian father, and for that, too, I thank You. When he was twelve years old he was working as a lumberjack in the forests, like a man. An old photo shows him with his axe on his shoulder and his pipe clamped between his teeth, a child among workers three or four times as old as him, and he doesn't look any sadder than the others. A few winters later, he decided that if he ever had children, they wouldn't leave home at the age of twelve to work their fingers to the bone with the men and the horses. He looked for a teacher to marry. He wanted the mother of his children to know the necessary words to make them like the books that instruct you. He didn't find a teacher, but he met a young girl who had beautiful handwriting. He married her, but he warned her that if ever You came to take her away, he'd start looking again for a teacher. His first wife died a few years later. Then our father went and asked our mother, who was a teacher, if she would marry him.

Whatever becomes of me later in life, I'll never be able to do any harm as long as I remember that our father, when he was still a child, was a lumberjack among other lumberjacks, who were swallowed up by a distant forest. Thank You, God, for giving me a French-Canadian father. Though You could have given me one who doesn't smoke as much as he does. His car reeks of cigarette ashes.

He's very fond of politics, our father. Thank You, God, for giving us French-Canadian politicians. After listening to their fine speeches, the French-Canadian people feel stronger in the land of America. Some of their speeches have been so fine that they've been printed in books. My friend Henri Laberge and I learned one of them by heart, like a prayer. At recess, we go to the end of the schoolyard, we climb up the hill, and there on the heights, in the wind that stirs the sparkling snow and burns our ears, using the words of a great politician from the past, we talk to the people who one day will hear us. Our speeches are so beautiful that our hearts get all excited in our chests. Sometimes tears come to our eyes. My friend Henri Laberge and I will become great politicians. He makes finer speeches than I do, but the people don't like to elect anyone who makes speeches that are too fine. When I become Prime Minister, I won't forget that it was the snow and the wind that listened to me first.

I thank You, God, for all the French people who didn't dare to become French Canadians. They were afraid of the sea and Canada doesn't need fearful people. I thank You for my ancestor who arrived here from France three centuries ago with nothing in his bag except a hammer and a chisel for cutting stone. He came to build churches in the valley of the St. Lawrence. Thank You for all the French Canadians who spread out across the entire territory of America. Thank You for the millions of French Canadians who emigrated to the United States and who pronounce their names now as if they were foreign. Thank You, God, for the French-Canadian nuns and missionaries who poured into the pagan regions of the earth to spread the news of Your existence. Thank You for the French-Canadian soldiers who died in wars far from their country, not knowing that their names would be inscribed on monuments. Thank You for the French-Canadian *coureurs des bois*; they followed the paths of the Indians and they didn't look down on either their language or their women.

Thank You, God, for having me be born a French Canadian, because our people have never caused harm to another people.

Roch
Carrier

11

Prayer of the Car that Is Travelling a Little Too Fast

Now that the car has slowed down, I'm saying a quick prayer to You, God, just in case You exist. The likelihood of Your existence seems to diminish as I study the things a person has to know in order to form an opinion about the world.

Why don't You make life a little easier for humans who believe in You? Let us have a look at You! No one's ever caught a glimpse of Your face, not even our grandfather Noah. Abraham heard Your voice, but You were hidden by a cloud, like Zorro behind his mask.

A Jesuit preacher assured us that the proof of Your existence resides in the fact that, throughout history, humans have believed in the existence of a supreme Being. For centuries, humans didn't believe that the automobile existed, yet it does . . . Public opinion doesn't create the truth. Here's another argument: let's suppose, God, that no human being believes in You. Is human unbelief the proof of Your non-existence? Then why should their belief in You be proof that You do exist?

Am I thinking too much? I feel as if I've drunk four bottles of beer. Am I drunk from thinking? I think I drank three bottles . . . Maybe four . . .

It's strange, all these ideas have come to me since the car slowed down. Does my brain work better at a slower speed? A few minutes ago we were driving along at a hundred miles an hour. I wasn't thinking about anything except how enjoyable it was to go so fast. I didn't doubt Your existence. Do we have to drive at high speeds to believe in You?

Our friend Roger is allowed to drive his father's Chrysler. We're on holidays. It's summer. Today, Sunday, there was a wrestling match in the Beauce. We filled the car. There are six of us. Everyone's here: Roger, Lapin, Bébé, Ti-Blanc,

Ti-Noir . . . Just boys. We want to be free, without the problems girls cause. When there are girls we aren't friends in the same way. They don't like us to drink beer.

We are free men, we've drunk beer, and we've applauded Johnny Rougeau, the French-Canadian champion. Our athlete was defending the honour of our race against Joe "The Killer" Christie.

While Johnny had his back turned to wave to his fans, The Killer snuck up and attacked. Johnny defended himself. The Killer threw some illegal powder into his eyes. For the first time in his career, we saw our champion cry. From pain. The powder burned his eyes like fire. Blinded and groping as if it were night, our champion spotted The Killer by the way his leather boots creaked on the floor of the ring. Finally, Johnny Rougeau gave The Killer a hammering that must have discouraged all the enemies of the French Canadians.

After Johnny's victory, we had our picture taken together, the six friends. Roger, Lapin,

Bébé, Ti-Blanc, Ti-Noir, me . . . We stood close together, each with one arm hooked around the shoulders of the one next to us.

We'd have liked to have our great Johnny Rougeau too, but no one was brave enough to ask him to come and pose with us. Oh, we'd have stuck out our chests for the camera! We may be shy, but we've got our pride. Johnny Rougeau is a very great champion, but we aren't dogshit! Roger wants to be a dentist who'll repair our people's decayed teeth; Lapin wants to be an architect and put up buildings for the government, while I'm going to be either a great universal poet or Prime Minister of Canada.

In a few years, God, I'll be a champion too . . . So why did You plant in my soul the idea that I have to do something important? My friends don't suffer from that urge. They're simply advancing towards the front door of real life, and unlike me, they're not burdened by a weighty baggage of dreams. Like great heavy butterflies, they're enjoying themselves in the wind. They have no desire to fly somewhere else.

They're satisfied with the air they breathe every day. Why do I want to become someone I'm not? Why do I want to become someone greater than I am? I feel as if You haven't finished creating me. I have to complete Your creature and improve him.

I don't accept life as You gave it to me. I dream of a different life. I often maintain that You've chosen me to be responsible for a great destiny. Excuse me, God, for losing my humility.

I would advise You to blame our father. He's the one who put it into my little child's head that if you don't become Prime Minister of Canada it's not worth going to school. If every father pushes his son to become Prime Minister, we're heading for a fine national disaster. The same thing for You, God: when I see the way the world turns, I hope that You're the only member of Your species. Too many generals is no good for war and it's bad for peace.

As I've already told You, I wasn't thinking about anything at all while our car was travelling at a hundred and ten miles an hour. The music of "Rock Around the Clock" was pouring out the windows onto the green fields decorated with daisies and black-and-white cows. After the photo without Johnny Rougeau, the group got back in Roger's father's Chrysler. Unlike the rest of us, Roger is allowed to sit on the paternal throne and hold the sacred wheel. To the rest of us that's still forbidden. I'm not allowed to even touch my father's coach with my finger. He'd have a heart attack and complain about it for a long time.

After Johnny Rougeau's triumph over Killer Christie, we headed back to our village. If there wasn't anything to do that evening, we'd go and watch the girls dance. That's one of the beautiful things in life, God, admiring their legs as they fling them around in time to the music. Their hips wiggle. Their skirts wriggle around their thighs. Their crinolines pirouette. Their hair waves like leaves caressed by a breeze that's gliding between the branches. Most of all, we observe the way their pointed chests jiggle. According to Your priests at the Petit Séminaire, we're committing a sin when we gaze at Your creatures. According to them, it would be better for our eternal salvation if we looked at the nails in the floor instead. Your priests teach that You are perfect. If they're right, everything You've made is perfect too. So why should it be a sin to admire the perfection of Your creatures when they fling themselves around on the dance floor? Why should it be a sin to want to hold such perfection in our arms while we listen to a mushy ballad by Pat Boone? Since You, God, are perfect, You don't have pimples on Your chin. So You must be braver than we are about asking girls to dance.

At first we were going forty miles an hour. We were obeying the road signs. We were far from the Milky Way, God. We were on a country road that the government covered with gravel, not asphalt, that has humps and curves and bumps because the farmers on either side voted against the Right Party.

I think it was me who threw out the challenge to Roger: "Are you brave enough to push the Chrysler up to a hundred miles an hour?" Right away, it was as if that car had been kicked in the rear. The tires threw off a volley of pebbles. The car sprang over the hill. We watched the needle climb up the numbers on the speedometer. We were tossed around like the travellers in the rocket in Jules Verne's *From the Earth to the Moon*. Soon the needle would reach seventy-five miles an hour. We kept saying: "Faster! Faster!" We were doing eighty; the dust from the gravel was far behind us. At eighty miles an hour Roger wasn't afraid. The needle kept climbing. The automobile was no longer on the gravel, it was hopping from hill to hill, from knoll to knoll, like a great metal kangaroo, while we had the stunned looks of little kangaroos in their mothers' pockets. We were up to a hundred miles an hour.

"Roger, are you scared to go a hundred and ten?"

Forgive me, God. I was the one who asked that stupid question. Our behinds felt something pushing under the car seat. We realized that

Roger was brave. I closed my eyes because I couldn't stand to see the spruce trees and the hydro poles rushing towards us so fast. Also, I didn't want to see my friends' fear. Yet I was as excited as if I'd taken off for Your sky. Never in my life had I moved at such a speed. I thought that never since the beginning of the world, whenever that was, had anyone in my family ever attained such a fabulous speed.

All at once, behind my closed eyes, it seemed to me that the Chrysler had left the ground. On the radio, Elvis Presley was singing "Blue Suede Shoes." The bumps, the humps were no longer shaking the car. The gravel was no longer creaking under the tires. Something like a big hammer struck the car. The bones in our bodies clattered together in our skeletons. I thought to myself: "We're dead!"

Then I opened my eyes. We'd landed in a field. The Chrysler was floating amid the daisies like a frog in a lily-pond. Before us stretched the blue lake, You know the one, at the curve in the road, where the boys and girls go to kiss in the moonlight. Roger had missed the curve. Thank You, God, for creating the lumberjacks who felled the trees in that place. If they'd forgotten a few maples, we'd have been turned into jam.

If You saved our lives, I thank You for it. It could be the proof that You exist. And if You don't exist, I'd like to tell You this: Dying at a hundred miles an hour might be better than living at ten.

Prayer of the Sin
I'd Have Liked
to Commit

If I still believed in You, God, I'd have a prayer to send You because I tried to succumb to temptation and commit a big sin. I ought to ask You to forgive me, but I'm not going to confess anything tonight, because I know that You don't exist. You're nothing but a dream in the minds of people who need You to explain the Universe. I, though, have chosen science. It helps me understand the way life operates. Science isn't like Inspector Maigret or Hercule Poirot; it doesn't clear up all the riddles, but a century or two from now, humans will be able to visit the Moon. And then science will know as much about the heavenly mysteries as You do.

You'd prefer it if I spoke to You with the humility of the shepherd who knows about nothing but his sheep and the star in the Big

Dipper that he sleeps under. I received a certain amount of intelligence from You. I've been studying at the Petit Séminaire for the past six years. So don't be surprised if I do a little thinking ... And the more I think, the fewer reasons I find for Your existence. Just between You and me, though, You and Your non-existence aren't the only things I think about. I've got other matters to reflect on.

Ever since she arrived for her holidays, Zouzou has been taking up quite a lot of space in my aquarium of ideas. From the front or the back, in her pink or green or yellow dress, she walks as if she were naked in Amazonia. You haven't seen Zouzou lying on the beach: the entire earth was her bed and the sky her blanket. I gaze at what I can see and I imagine what I can't. I shudder before so much beauty. I almost want to start believing in You again. She's an angel fallen from Heaven onto a humble beach on our planet. With my eyes focussed on her body, I thought about You: "God," I said to myself, "is the only artist with the power to sculpt a statue that makes people dizzy every time the statue's chest is lifted by the breath of life."

How I wished I were the soul that inhabited that body! On the beach, Zouzou was offering herself completely to the breeze and to everything that exists. I was as close as I could be, but far away, so far, in a chair. I'd have been so happy to be the sand beneath her back, the sun on her pretty round belly, the air she was breathing, the July wind. Zouzou! Ah, Zouzou! Oh, Zouzou! It is possible to be awake yet dream all night, whispering that name . . .

Every day, I waited for her to appear on the beach. When she undoes her dress to reveal her body striped by a red bikini, she's like a butterfly in the earthly paradise. Her white skin, not yet browned by the sun, glows like a pearl when its oyster is opened. Zouzou dazzles like the ray of dawn when it pierces the dusky wall of night. (Thank You, God, for giving me the gift of poetry.)

Gazing like that made me breathless, as if I'd climbed the stairs to the top of the Empire State

Building in New York. My heart was panicking. My blood was bubbling in my arteries. I was proud to be a boy and to feel the kind of burning that makes you shiver as if you were cold... In Your day, God, You weren't modern enough to have those sensations!

Yesterday, Zouzou was stretched out on the beach, as usual. She knelt down; her body pivoted on her knees as she offered her whipped-cream boobs to the four points of the compass, and then she sat. That was when her legs parted and in the poplars all around there was a sudden hush: the swallows fell silent and the leaves restrained themselves from trembling. Finally, closing her legs with delight, she lay down on her back.

I admired that ballet as I would have admired an unreal flower that had blossomed before my eyes.

I listen to myself praying, God, and I thank You for granting me the privilege of reading the great immortal authors. Without them, I would never have known how to talk about a moment of grace. A man needs to have style, because "the style is the man."

I admired in silence. Like the bull fascinated by the torero's red cape, I was dazzled by Zouzou's bikini. She was as desirable as gold is to the poor, as water is to the summer traveller lost in the Gobi desert, as Heaven is to those who believe in You. Under the red bikini so much secret beauty was hidden. The thought of it paralyzed me. I was breathless. Of everything that I could see around me, only Zouzou was breathing. I had no voice. The moment was extraordinary. How did I manage to approach her and say:

"Would you like to go for a boat ride?"

"Only if you do the rowing . . ."

"I'll row there and back."

To sit close to Zouzou, I'd have rowed on the land itself if she had asked me. I was proud that I'd said what I'd said. Not even the poet Lamartine, on the shore of his famous lake, had spoken more elegantly.

Once the blue rowboat had been pushed into the water, Zouzou got inside. I was ogling her.

Because of her eyes, I thought she looked a little like a hare caught in a trap. Was she familiar with Lamartine, the great poet, who for the rest of his life never forgot a ride he'd taken in a rowboat on a lake? I asked her. A girl that beautiful isn't obliged to know everything. I explained to her that Lamartine lived a long time ago. She replied that there are times when she feels old.

I planted the two oars in the soft, soft water. Because Zouzou had agreed to accompany me in my skiff, I was going to make this glide across our own lake's shimmering deep so beautiful she'd remember it forever. Like an angel in a red bikini, Zouzou would visit the dreams of the prince of poets that I, like Ronsard, was going to become.

She sat in the prow, majestic, the statue of a Greek divinity become living woman, and I was rowing. The lake was a mirror of tranquillity. The sun blazed as it strove to light up the nights of unfathomable space, and the water reflected that cosmic conflagration. I was dazed. Was it the light that was irritating my eyes? Was it Zouzou, unreal and yet so close to me? Held back forcibly by her frail garment, her breasts, like an oppressed people, aspired to their liberation. Her thighs, squeezed tightly together, sometimes opened. I looked away. Vertigo took hold of me as it will do when I first gaze on Niagara Falls.

Soon the sun would return to its nest of shadows, to sleep. It seemed to me that the lake, though calm, was heaving like a sea under a gale. My heart was throbbing as if it were the heart of the entire world . . . You gave me the soul of a poet, God, don't deny it!

Captain of my rowboat, I veered to port. I knew a beach shaded by poplars with leaves that make a hushing sound. No one had built a cabin there yet. It was impossible not to be alone there. It would be more beautiful than a dream. Zouzou and I would be part of nature like Adam and Eve—and her beauty wouldn't be buried in a bikini.

On our secluded beach, we weren't really alone. The breeze in the leaves accompanied us, along with the delicate lapping of the water and the scent of the shade beneath the trees. Our bodies were pulsating with youth. In the light that was fading little by little was reflected a far-off eternity. Along with us, there were bees that were drinking from the wildflowers' delicate cups. Above all, there was silence. Zouzou was lying beside me, but our silence was so profound that she seemed to be absent, on the opposite shore or even farther away, in the city of Quebec where she came from or even farther. And yet the warm flesh of her shoulder was touching mine. I kissed her mouth. It tasted like straw-berry ice cream. I kissed her again. Again. Several times. Again and again. (One day, God, I'll entitle one of my books *Again*.) My hand glided onto her belly and then ventured onto her breasts. It was blazing, it was soft, it was as poignant as if I were holding her heart, it was as unsettling as a sin.

If I still believed in You, I'd have got up then and there and raced away to throw myself at the feet of Your priest and confess. It felt so good! Under Zouzou's breast her heart was becoming as agitated as mine. I suggested:

"We should take our clothes off ... Have you heard of the Garden of Eden?"

"With all these mosquitoes eating me alive, it sure as hell isn't here."

"Then just let me see what's hidden inside your bathing suit."

She seemed slightly offended:

"No ... Not today ... Maybe tomorrow."

I put my hand inside the bikini. I wouldn't have felt any richer if I'd been holding a handful of diamonds.

I was drunk as if I'd drunk too much wine. Zouzou had said: "Maybe tomorrow ..." We got back in the boat. I was rowing. I was stupefied. She had said: "Maybe tomorrow . . ." I was strong. I could have rowed all night. Across the Atlantic. A young man becomes a giant when he's told: "Maybe tomorrow ..."

God, if the legend that You see everything is true, You know that during the night, in my dream, Zouzou was next to me, her body free of her bikini; the mosquitoes weren't pestering us. She had said: "Maybe tomorrow ..."

Today, my day in the swamp planting sur-
veyor's stakes was as long as the day of a slave.
Yet I was a free man. Before the sun had set,
Zouzou would board my frail craft and we would
sail towards Cythera, as a poet said, or towards
the extravagant shore, in the words of another.
God, You were going to find Zouzou and me clad
in a single moonbeam!

Unfortunately, I'm just a teenager, a poor student. There are so many books I still have to
read. I don't want to give life to a child. I still
feel lost on earth myself. I had to go to the drugstore. This town is small, so our drugstore is tiny.
It's run by the father of our friend, Big Labotte.
You have to watch out. Big Labotte's father is a
real joker. Big Labotte told us that his father
plays with condoms. He pierces them by sticking
pins through their protective envelopes.

God, have You ever gone into a drugstore to
buy condoms? It was my first time. Never before
had my little soldier needed to don parade uniform. Thanks to the good health You gave me
I'd never even been inside a drugstore. Thank

You for always protecting me from devastating germs. Zouzou had said: "Maybe tomorrow . . ." Tonight, I needed some sturdy condoms. Vesuvius was getting ready to erupt.

Big Labotte has a sister named Germaine. I won't give You a long explanation for why everybody calls her Fat Germaine. As I pushed open the door of the drugstore there she was behind the counter. Very prominent.

I hadn't foreseen this disaster. To ask her for condoms would be impossible. She'd broadcast it to the entire population of our town and beyond, by word of mouth and by telephone. She'd write it in her diary and to her correspondents in Europe and Africa. She greeted me majestically.

"What an honour! My brother's been talking about you for ages, but this is the first time I've seen you close enough to talk to. What do you want?"

To hell with my reputation! To hell with gossip! A great future awaits me, opening its rosy arms. I'd do it. I wasn't going to let the first obstacle overcome me. I needed condoms. I would ask for condoms.

"I'd like," I began with conviction, "I'd like some . . ." I hesitated. "I'd like some chocolates."

Germaine is fat. Germaine is a blabber-mouth. Germaine is greedy. I was forced to stay in the drugstore with her for over an hour. She kept delivering her news—local, regional and international. I pretended to be listening while I watched her devour my chocolates.

When I was finally able to free myself of the weight of Fat Germaine, without condoms and without chocolates, I raced towards the one who had told me: "Maybe tomorrow . . ."

Zouzou wasn't waiting for me. She'd gone off in the rowboat, I was told, that was heading left, towards the secret beach. At the oars was Big Labotte.

13

Prayer
after the
Great Election Speech

Their factory was shut down three months ago. The workers, their wives, their children, their families were all gathered in a big hangar. They listened to me. They applauded me. The Minister received less applause than I did. He told me himself, with his own mouth, that they liked my speech better than his. The Minister also confided that at my age he'd been so shy he couldn't say *papa* without stammering.

Let's construct a syllogism, God. It won't be too complicated. When he was eighteen, the Minister couldn't say two consecutive words to one person and the Minister became a Minister. At eighteen, I delivered a speech to two thousand persons, therefore I should become two thousand times as important as the Minister. The reasoning is logical.

While I spoke, the men applauded and the women wept. Yes, God, I made the mothers weep. Yet I don't feel proud. I ran away from my triumph and came to pray to You here in the car. The Minister is busy shaking hands. The workers' hands are clean because they're not working.

God, You gave me eloquence. But tonight You must wish You hadn't given me that gift. The men applauded. The women had tears in their eyes. Because of the flowered hats the mothers were wearing, the crowd was like a flowery field in our rugged Dorchester County. A number of them even got to their feet to applaud my speech, but tonight I feel like crying. It would relieve my soul.

Do I need to tell You how this whole business began? I've often declaimed the speeches of the great patriots, along with Henri Laberge, at the top of the hill behind the Petit Séminaire. Our voices would box with the wind. You made Henri more eloquent than me, but I'm the one who was chosen as official delegate from the Petit Séminaire to the provincial elocution contest in the city of Quebec. If You've read *L'Action catholique*, God, You already know that.

A few days after the oratorical competition in Quebec, the loudspeaker at the Petit Séminaire summoned me to the telephone, at once. All the time I've been at boarding school, no one's ever asked for me on the phone. Our mother prefers to write. Her letters always start out the same way: "Dear child, We at home are all well and I hope that you are too." Our mother spent her youth teaching grammar to the surly sons of farmers. She is still faithful to writing and she boycotts Alexander Graham Bell's invention. When our grandfather passed away, she announced the news by correspondence. By the time I received her letter, our grandfather was already buried and he'd had time to get to Purgatory on foot.

So when the loudspeaker made my name ring out in the sky above the Beauce, when I heard that I was wanted on the telephone, I deduced that some disaster graver than death had swooped down somewhere. I raced to the telephone booth. My heart was beating so hard it got there one and one-eighth seconds before I did.

"Hello, my boy!" exclaimed an unfamiliar voice. "I hear you make a hell of a fine speech..."

"Yes ... I delivered a speech in Quebec City..."

"My boy, you can't know because it's still a state secret, but the Right Party is about to call an election ... When we call an election, we intend to win. Otherwise it wouldn't be worth bothering people. What do you think about that?"

"That's democracy... I've studied the history of the ancient Greeks..."

"Them too, the Greeks, they do like everybody else: they call elections to win them. Losing an election, that's anti-democratic ... Now, my boy, let me tell you why I'm going out of my way to talk to you. I have the responsibility of being the head political organizer for the Right Party in this riding. I know the Prime Minister's private phone number. I know him intimately. He knows the name of at least two of my eleven children. I know your father, too. He trusts me. He's gonna buy his next Ford from me. Now, your father's told me about you... See, I'm looking for a future Prime Minister of Canada. In our country we talk too much about old things from the past, when we oughtta be talking about the future. We aren't dead, for Christ's sake! The people want to hear about their future. At every political meeting I'm gonna give the youth of this country a chance to talk about the future. I need a future Prime Minister that's gonna talk about the future. Our party is the party of the future. It's the future that counts, goddamnit! Are you interested in becoming a future Prime Minister?"

A shrewd politician never reveals everything that's on his mind. Forgive me, God, but a politician removes his veils one at a time, like Lili Saint-Cyr the stripper. He should bring the other party around to revealing its intentions. So I told him:

"I'd have to think about it."

The voice exploded:

"Christ almighty! Are you interested in the future, yes or no?"

A shrewd politician doesn't allow himself to be impressed.

"I'm not old enough to vote yet . . ."

"Jesus! You don't need the right to vote to attack the Opposition. It's the Opposition that's threatening democracy in our province. Are you for democracy, yes or no? Do you want to become a future Prime Minister? . . . Your father and me, we had a talk, man to man. He wants a good price on his next Ford. The both of us are fathers, we understand each other . . . You're costing him plenty, my boy . . . He'll get that good price . . . and I'm gonna pay you well too. Besides that, here's some free advice: If you want to become a future Prime Minister, you'd better join the parade right now."

And that, God, is how politics came along and collared me.

Two weeks later, temporarily freed from the Petit Séminaire, along with our mother, our father, our brothers, our sister and the baby, I was waiting for the head political organizer in our riding. A long, shiny, black car came to a stop outside our house without stirring up even one particle of dust. It was for me. I got in and drove away, waving like a real Prime Minister. Our family had already elected me.

Like a real Prime Minister, I went over the pages of my speech in the limousine. I explained to the voters why they should re-elect the Right Party. I listed all the woes that would destroy the province of Quebec if the population chose the Opposition. The head political organizer had given me some red cards that listed all those disasters. I added a few; I wanted to show him that I didn't need his red cards to understand politics.

As for the rest . . . You know how events unfolded. The limousine stopped at the door to the hangar. On the other side there was a sea of cars. I had to convince all those people assembled in the hangar not to vote for the Opposition.

Someone opened the door for me. Big round men with wrinkled pants and tight neckties welcomed me as if I were the Prime Minister. I didn't know any of them. They were so fat they looked as if they were the cause of famine in the poor countries. They said to me: "We hear you make a hell of a fine speech!" They congratulated me by punching my shoulders with their fists. After that came a chorus of distinguished ladies reeking of perfume. Their smiles seemed to be whispering: "When you've finished your speech, we'll let you touch our boobs." (Excuse me, God, for that depraved thought.)

I was led to the stage where a microphone was waiting and it was waiting for my speech. Two rows of leading citizens—mayors, school board chairmen, churchwardens, Caisse Populaire managers, and Grand Knights of the Order of Columbus—were already seated to lend their lustre to the event, as they say. The Minister in the flesh arrived last, just after me. He took pains to shake every one of the outstretched hands, including mine, and said to me: "Welcome to the winning team!" Shaking hands is important in politics.

My chair was next to the Minister's. He leaned across and said into my ear:

"We're sure of victory, but we need all men of good will if we're going to beat the Opposition. If the Opposition gets hold of power, it would be ten times worse than Communism!"

I assured him that my speech was going to bomb the Opposition and cause damage. He congratulated me.

"The Right Party needs a young fella like you."

The Minister himself was showing his great confidence in me. I promised myself he wouldn't be disappointed.

My gaze turned to the crowd. I spotted our father right away, far back in the crowd. His cigarette was pointing upwards: that's a sign that he's nervous. I was surprised to see him. He'd told me he couldn't come to this meeting.

So he'd let me drive off in my limousine and followed along in his Ford. Our father didn't want to ride with me. He's so independent. He preferred to hold the wheel himself instead of being driven. Something must be wrong. Our father didn't go to school for very long. He was a humble lumberjack. He didn't dare to sit beside a future Prime Minister, not even his own son. I'm not proud. A Prime Minister who intimidates his own father isn't much of a man.

The crowd was filling the vast hangar. The factory has been shut down. They don't produce buses any more. There are no more buses to crowd together. The hangar was empty. They were able to bring in a crowd of voters, in the place of the buses. It was a peaceful crowd, as placid as a lake. A fog of tobacco smoke was creeping over their heads. As if they were going to mass, the men were in their Sunday suits. They were waiting. They were silent. They were smoking.

I could sense what they were thinking about, God. Would there be work in their factory again some day? How long would they be able to buy food? Winter was coming soon; they'd have to buy clothes for their children who grow from season to season. Would they have to move their families? Where? And where would they find work for their arms? Was there any in town? If so, they'd have to sell their houses. Who'd want to buy a house in this village where everyone is trying to sell their houses? Is town a good place for bringing up children? According to the paper, there are already a lot of jobless men in town. And they don't speak English. In town, you have to know how to speak English ... Will they be condemned to sit and wait, with their elbows on the kitchen table, till old age comes along and death takes them away, leaving behind a wife who won't have lived a life that lets you walk with your head held high?

The women were wiping the tears on their cheeks with their little white handkerchiefs. They could read what was on their men's minds.

The Minister stepped up to the microphone. The crowd applauded the way an ocean roars. He waited humbly till they fell silent. Then he opened his arms and the loudspeakers projected his voice all the way to the mountains of Belle-chasse. He talked about me, a boy who knows nothing about life aside from the books he's read. My heart was thumping the way it does when I dance too close to a girl.

"My dear friends, I am going to introduce

to you a child of our people, a well-brought-up young man who's going to speak the truth to you as he stands at the threshold of a brilliant political career. I'm going to introduce to you a young man who's honest, sincere and forthright. Listen closely to what he has to say. This young man is going to tell you, in words you'll understand, why you have to tell the Opposition to go to hell. This forthright young man is going to explain to you why you should vote for me, your servant, your MP, your Minister, your friend, your big brother. Now without further delay, I want you to welcome this young man, a future Prime Minister of Canada!"

That's how the Minister talked about me.

As I made my way to the microphone, I felt the platform under my feet like a raft on a tumultuous sea. I hadn't said a word yet but already they were listening to me. The women were holding back their tears. The men weren't smoking. They were looking me up and down. They were anxious to hear my first words. There were two thousand of them.

A few months earlier, this shed had been crammed with new buses. A few months earlier, these men had been working and complaining to their wives that they were tired. Today, they were even more tired, but they weren't working.

The lesson of the riding's head political organizer came back to me: We call elections to win them. I was thinking that a good politician is one who harvests bushels of votes. And I believe that a good speaker is one who doesn't need the pages of a written speech.

"*Mesdames, mesdemoiselles, messieurs*, the Right Party wants the factories to operate and the workers to work." (Thunderous applause, a hurricane of Yes! Yes! rolled over me.) "Unfortunately, your factory is no longer operating. You are no longer working. Your buses no longer set off across the vast roads of North America. That is a human catastrophe. A national catastrophe. And it's the Opposition's fault! You must vote against the Opposition."

The entire crowd, men and women, young and old, rose to their feet as one. Their anger was powerful. If a representative of the Opposition had been present, they'd have torn him to pieces. Then they calmly resumed their seats. I wanted that powerful crowd to rise up again. I went on:

"Now listen carefully to what I'm going to say. I have been charged with bringing you some great news. I am putting my own political future at stake because I believe in what I'm about to tell you. After the election, the Right Party is going to reopen your factory! The day after the Right Party is elected, I give you my personal commitment that I will come here and put the key to the factory in the hand of your mayor."

You saw the crowd, God, come rolling towards me like a sea. You saw the tears flow like rivers. You saw the workers' broad, thick hands applauding as if these people had witnessed a miracle.

I went back to my seat. The Minister congratulated me.

"Good thing you decided to stop talking, or they'd've voted for you instead of me."

He turned towards another MP and I heard him say:

"That little bugger understands politics . . . He already knows that nobody's obliged to keep an election promise."

I didn't say anything more. I didn't listen to anything more. The limousine is bringing me back home. The driver said: "You got the makings of a Prime Minister, my boy!" Our father's Ford must be following us. My heart is as heavy as the heart of a child who's spilled the milk on the tablecloth.

Forgive me, God, for lying to some honest workers who like fine speeches. I don't want to be Prime Minister of Canada any more.

14

Prayer for the
Very Great Poet
of the Americas

It's flagrant, it's patently obvious: I am going to be the greatest poet between the Atlantic Ocean and the Pacific, and I warn you, God, I'll soon stop praying to You.

To tell You the truth, my urge to rebel isn't very strong and I don't have much to criticize You for. Between You and me, the Universe is rather awe-inspiring and the unknown world must be even more captivating. Unfortunately, You don't forbid wars and You don't wipe out diseases that torture those You've created. Why do You condemn to death those in whom You've implanted a desire for eternity? Why do You tolerate poverty? It deprives of food millions of children to whom You've given a stomach! Aside from those flaws, God, You're a pretty good guy.

Still, if I want to become a great poet, I have to do as the great poets do and rebel against You. Recently I've read, in hiding from the priests, some of the best poets of the modern era. The more poets believe in You, the less good their poetry is. That's my conclusion. Now, since I have to rebel, I'm going to rebel. Starting very soon, I want You to know that I'm going to become an unbeliever, a skeptic, an infidel, a pagan. I ask You to forgive me in advance, God.

Since I've thrown open the floodgates of poetry, every poem I write is another feather added to my poet's wings. Their wingspan stretches right across my back. My soul is becoming as vast as the entire world. A poet is an explorer who has the power to soar above unknown and lofty zones. I am becoming like those angels I used to believe in, back when I used to pray to You . . . I don't believe in Your angels any more.

The secret notebook that I keep hidden under my mattress in the dormitory contains a hundred and thirty-eight poems. My classmates mustn't find out that I'm a poet. They'd think I was weird like Baudelaire, dissolute like Byron (who also had a clubfoot), a reprobate like Villon, wacko like Rimbaud. I'd be kicked off our basketball team.

I've sent some of my compositions to newspapers and magazines. People don't know how to read poetry nowadays. No one understood my poems. They all refused to publish them. They prefer the old lines in bad poems by poets already dead who they think are still alive. Their rejections don't surprise me. The most illustrious poets in history have been banned. Which says a lot about freedom of expression!

You drivelling old fogies at *Le Devoir*, *La Presse*, *La Revue d'Amérique française*, *L'Action catholique*, I thank you for turning down my work. Heavenly Father, bless those ancient skulls that are like closets that haven't been opened for a hundred years. By rejecting my poems they've given me dazzling proof that my poetry is new, revolutionary and maybe immortal.

You who have the power to read over my

157

Prayer for
the Very
Great Poet
of the
Americas

shoulder, You know that no one has ever used the language as elegantly as I have to write about the beauty of the fir trees and their garlands of snow. I've also written magnificent poems about the rain which "spreads a veil of mystery between the present moment and eternity." Nor have You forgotten my disturbing poem about the November wind that "creeps across the earth, identical to man, knowing not whence he comes nor whither he is going." My best poem is probably the one in which I write that "sorrow weighs on human souls like a stone at the bottom of the sea, but the sea is free of suffering from not understanding its fate."

There's another poem that will certainly earn me a photograph in the *Dictionnaire des grand poètes universels*: the ode that was inspired by Hélène's betrayal. I caught her skating with my mortal enemy, Charlot Cheval. She was smiling as if she were with me. All the great poets have suffered because of their unfaithful muse. The pain on that occasion helped me produce a hundred and nineteen lines.

No one wanted to publish my poetry. Thank You, God, for that privilege. It's a sign that You've drawn on the horizon for me. The great poets are misunderstood. Great poetry is banned. Mediocrity controls the brains of man. Only poets who are misunderstood become famous.

The other day, I asked the monitor's permission to consult the doctor about a sexual matter. If it's about sex, the monitor gives his permission immediately. If it's about cancer or sudden death, you have to wait weeks for him to sign the permission form.

Instead of going to the doctor, I took my poetry notebook and hitchhiked into town, where there's a printer. In his printshop, I lit my poet's pipe and he lit his—the pipe of an old printer. We chewed the fat. When our pipes went out, the old printer undertook to print twenty-eight pages of my purest poetry. Then he put on his round eyeglasses and, on a beautiful white sheet of paper, he wrote me a certificate of good sexual health. On my return, the monitor read it closely and conceded: "Very well. And don't forget to confess as often as you need to."

Soon my name will be inscribed upon the cover of a book, like Homer, Victor Hugo, Verlaine, Ronsard and Alfred DesRochers. I'll be an author! People will learn my poems by heart, they'll recite them in public. Those poems will describe the author's extraordinary life . . . My life has to become extraordinary! Now I just had to pay the printer's bill. He couldn't extend credit to poetry. The old printer demanded a lot of money, but no doubt he's an honest man because he shared his tobacco with me.

I no longer believe in miracles. It's impossible to turn water into wine. It's impossible to transform an empty wallet into one that's full.

Would I dare to ask our father for financial support? His future Prime Minister of Canada had withdrawn to bestride Pegasus. It wouldn't make him proud. When our mother informed him that I'd become a poet, he wanted to know if I was very sick.

So instead, I decided to work by the sweat of my brow . . .

June arrived, with its flowers, its girls in light dresses and our summer holidays. All I had to do was find work. You, God, gave me intelligence, You gave me imagination, but all those years I spent at the Petit Séminaire turned me into an extraterrestrial. The real world before me resembles a city with a wall around it. I have no idea what we must do in order to live on the other side of that wall.

That book was important to me. I gathered up every shred of courage and went to a moving company. The manager told me: "I'd trust you with a box of pencils on a staircase, but not with my Frigidaire." He advised me to check out the hotels.

From village to village, from inn to inn, I offered my smile and the good manners I'd learned at the Petit Séminaire. It was painful, humiliating, for a great poet to beg for work.

Finally, I was needed in a country tavern. The customers have chests as broad as the front of their trucks. Their arms are like the undressed lumber they haul to the sawmills. Saturdays are

for parties. They polish the nickel-plated orna-
ments on their vehicles as if they were fine sil-
ver, then they go to the tavern, their trucks
roaring like rutting beasts. To impress the girls,
the customers unbutton their shirts. And who
wouldn't be impressed by such hairy chests?
Their rolled-up sleeves reveal biceps swollen

like tires.

When they sit at a table, my customers don't
expect a smile steeped in Platonic philosophy.
They couldn't care less if I were the greatest poet
in North and South America combined. They're
parched. Like a herd of thirsty oxen, they moo
in the direction of the waiter.

"Hey, ya little fucker, bring me a beer."

What they hate most is a glass. My first night
on the job, I brought a customer a glass. He bit
into it as if it were a piece of pie and spat out
some crumbs . . . So, no glasses for the beer, just
bottles on the table. Not small ones either!
Small bottles, like glasses, are for pansies. My
customers tolerate only big ones. Finally, they
aren't satisfied unless the entire surface of the

table is covered. It has to be impossible for the waiter to add even one.

God, they've inherited the thirst of our grandfather Noah who planted his vine in the Bible. They consume as much fuel as their trucks laden with maple trees when they climb Mont Orignal.

God, I didn't come here to make my fortune. As soon as I've scraped together the amount I need, I'll go back to see the old printer who is going to make my first book. I could also become a very great businessman, because I have a definite instinct for profit.

Here's what I've discovered. If my customer gets the bill before he drinks his first beer, he can read the total as precisely as a notary. But if my customer receives the bill after he's drunk all his beer, his eyesight is blurry; he's not very interested in imitating his notary. Finally, if the customer asks for even more beer to quench his cosmic and ancestral thirst, he'll soon be totally blind. So you just have to be patient and wait for the harvest. Does the bill read thirty dollars and sixty-three cents? I can tell them forty-three sixty-three and even sixty-three forty-three, if it's very late. The customer trusts me the way he trusts his notary.

That was how I took my first steps along the road of finance. Like that other great poet in his day, François Villon, I too have robbed passersby, decent truckers from the counties of Beauce, Dorchester and Frontenac, where our father was born. Forgive me, God, for becoming a business-man. That's where Pegasus has brought me.

No, I don't regret having plundered a tipsy customer. Thanks to that tax, my first book is going to be printed. Otherwise, the truckers would have drunk even more beer and their money, instead of being transmuted into poetic gems, would have become worthless piss. (Whoops! Sorry, God.)

Thank You for granting me the power of poetry. Thank You for allowing me to print my first book. When I think about the truckers, I ask You to give me a little remorse.

15

Prayer of the
Young Man of the Future
Who Is On His Way
to the City

God, I've done a lot of thinking. If You existed, I'd argue with You, and I could convince You that You don't exist. I have no more doubts. But because I'm a good sport and a good boy, I'm going to send You another little prayer.

I've leafed through a good many books. One of them advised me to drop everything, saying that before you turn twenty, you must take the road that leads to the place you dream of going to on this earth.

This morning, I was standing at the side of the road. I was hitchhiking. Destination: New York. I was emigrating like my uncles and my cousins whom You watched as they went to the United States. You saw them come back, too, with gold teeth, and cars with rear ends as long as that, and American words that crackled inside their French language.

As soon as I got there I would climb to the top of the Empire State Building. I'd gaze out at the city below the way you study the water in a lake before diving in. Then I would fill my lungs with the air of New York and, like Rastignac, the hero of a novel by Balzac which I've read three times, I would declare: "To the two of us, New York!"

My uncles and my cousins took with them in their suitcases heavy woollen socks, a Catholic missal and a rosary. Our father, when he went away, took his axe, his whetstone and his pipe. As for me, my suitcase held paper, dictionaries, a book of Rimbaud's poems, a thin volume of Villon and some paper on which I'd copied out "Easter in New York" and some paragraphs from *The Trans-Siberian*, by Blaise Cendrars. I also brought a few copies of my first book.

It wasn't even a village: just a church, a saw-mill and three or four houses. No one came along except flies, ants, a few butterflies, some grasshoppers and a cart full of hay being pulled by an old mare. The master had forgotten to get in himself.

I'd been waiting for more than an hour where two country roads formed a cross beneath a sky inhabited by vacationing birds. Now and then, a daisy in the field was stirred by the fleeting passage of a groundhog.

Eventually, a vehicle drove up. Bright as a comet. I brandished my thumb. He didn't slow down. It was a sparkling red convertible, a sports car, one of those racing cars that don't stop for a hitchhiker with a suitcase, even if it's full of poetry. Yet the machine came to a halt almost in front of me, accompanied by a cyclone and a hail of pebbles.

"Where do you go on foot like that?" asked the driver who was wearing a flat, checkered cap and dark aviator's glasses.

"New York."

"You'll be walk then, I'm go to Montreal, Canada."

167

Prayer of the
Young Man
of the Future
Who Is On
His Way
to the City

The motor was already rumbling, the pistons were swollen with energy, the chassis was quivering with impatience: the rocket was going to take off without me. I'd never been in a sports car. Before the dream vanished, I shouted louder than the orchestra of its turbines:

"I think I've changed my mind; I'll go to Montreal instead."

And that, God, was how I started out for New York, in the United States, and then headed for Montreal, in Canada. There are those who will conclude that it doesn't take much to make me change my mind. "A mere car can turn him off his course," they will say; "he allows his destiny to drift like a snowflake in a squall." Those people are mistaken. You have equipped me with a proud will that doesn't bend like an alder. Besides, I'm a poet, and the poet can read signs that are invisible to the rest of the world. The sports car that had stopped on my road was obviously one of them.

"And what you will do in the big city?" asked the driver with his heavy accent.

"What am I going to do?"

I repeated his question to give myself time to prepare my answer.

"I'm going to write poetry, Monsieur."

The jaws of his brakes gripped as if a cow had fallen from the sky across the road. The tires groaned, the car reared up, then shuddered to a stop like a plough that's been jammed by a stone in the soil.

169

Prayer of the
Young Man
of the Future
Who Is On
His Way
to the City

"Get out this minute!" ordered the angry driver.

I noticed that he had big arms.

"I said to get out!"

Thunderstruck by his sudden anger, I didn't move.

"Montreal's got too much poets, too much good-for-nothing. Montreal's got too much feelings. What we want in Montreal is builders, businessmen, gamblers, risk-takers, inventors, pirates, bandits: people to do something. Not poets. Out!"

I liked that sports car. I brought up another plan.

"Our father wants me to become the Prime Minister of Canada."

"Son of a redheaded whore! If you're candidate to be Prime Minister, I, Tommy Papoulakis, I vote against you for sure. A traveller on foot that wants to be Prime Minister! Are you wanting everybody to travel on foot like you?"

I pushed the door and meekly got out of the car.

"Hold on there!"

I turned around. He took off his dark glasses. He gazed at me for a moment. I could feel his eyes passing through me like a fork through a piece of meat.

"Son of a redheaded whore! When I think about all the no-goods in politics, I think you can be Prime Minister. When that happens, you'll remember that Tommy Papoulakis kicked you the hell out of his sports car when you were starting out in your life; you'll be government, you'll be boss, and then you can bankrupt my business . . . But if I take you to Montreal now, free for nothing, in my beautiful convertible, you'll remember Tommy Papoulakis a nice man, so then if you become Prime Minister, when I phone to congratulate, you won't wait till I ask for a favour, you give me one. Get on board!"

I settled my behind into the leather seat that was as soft as the skin of a damsel's breast. The car took off like Jules Verne's rocket heading for the Moon. On either side of our spaceship, spruce trees, haystacks, cows, barns and houses sped by.

"Are you tell me the truth? Does your father really want you to be Prime Minister?"

"Yes, Monsieur."

"Son of a redheaded whore! If you're all the time polite like that, you won't get elected to your parish council . . . Now tell me truth: Do *you* really want to be Prime Minister?"

I wanted to continue this trip in a sports car; it wasn't the time to talk about poetry.

"Yes, our father thinks I'd be good at politics."

"Let me tell you little secret. In this life, a man has to do opposite of what his father tell him. Remember what Tommy Papoulakis

171

Prayer of the
Young Man
of the Future
Who Is On
His Way
to the City

told you ... What have you learned to be Prime Minister?"

"I've studied the classics, algebra, geometry, trigonometry, history, philosophy, literature ... Lots of subjects ... I forget some ...."

"You'll be well-educated Prime Minister all right, but one thing your priests didn't teach.

Now don't forget what Tommy Papoulakis tell you: what rules the world is the sex."

Politely, I protested such an extravagant idea. Life's a lot more complex than that. I enjoy crude words and coarse laughter. I'm a man and vulgarity gives a man pleasure. But I'm also a poet. While I may chortle at his off-colour stories, I would also like it if all words were stamped with the softness of the breeze on the perfume of leafy trees. Do you understand, God? When a person is crude, first I laugh, then I blush, and then a twinge in my belly urges me to reply:

"That's a good one, Monsieur Papoulakis, but you have to be objective. When a person's spent years studying the history of the world, you have to admit it's ideas that guide people as they evolve."

"Only thing I have to admit is that after all your study, you're still ignoramus. Son of a red-headed whore! Make some more studying. When you know a little more about life, you'll understand that the sex rules the world. Don't forget that. When you're Prime Minister, that principle will help you understand most complicated situations. The priests taught you to look at ideas, but I'm tell you: keep eye on sex life of the people that have ideas. Don't forget. And you'll thank Tommy Papoulakis for tell you."

"You don't become a great politician with an idea like that . . ."

"Son of a redheaded whore! Just be happy doing politics! After you're dead, others will decide if what you did was great, yes or no."

I was ill at ease. I was insulted, revolted by his simple-minded cynicism, by that simplistic view of the complex chemistry of individuals, peoples and history. I refused to spend one more minute with this uncouth individual. His crude certainty

173

Prayer of the
Young Man
of the Future
Who Is On
His Way
to the City

was an insult to the thinkers who have ennobled human intelligence. On the other hand—and I know that You'll understand me, God—that sports car was a marvel of twentieth-century technology. In that car you were already in the next century. It was exalting to feel the wind of freedom ruffling my poet's hair. The car was so powerful it could have flown away. But it was content to travel along the ground and give us the pleasure of hearing its tires whine like the airplanes that some day will be travelling faster than sound.

Just barely free of my Petit Séminaire, I was beginning my first day on the planet of real life. The most beautiful sports car in the country had driven out of a page in a magazine to pick me up along my country road. I was travelling towards my destiny. In spite of his obtuse ideas, in spite of his insults to my ideas, I decide not to desert my travelling companion.

"I'm tell you something else," Tommy Papoulakis went on. "You have to be watch out for books. Writing a book take time. The more

time writer spends with paper, the more he forget about life. The thicker the book, the more
mistake in it. To think too much is like drink too
much, eat too much, work too much, or sleep
too much. That's not where you'll find truth.
Truth is, everything a man do, he do to please
that little banana that hang between his two
legs. A man even be ready to die for that."

At the Petit Séminaire, we were trained to
demolish an opponent's arguments. I felt strong.
I was about to deal the fatal blow.

"You're right if you're talking about nature in
general. Nature has no goal but to ensure the
survival and propagation of the species. Man is
different, fortunately. You must distinguish man
from the other species. What characterizes man
is ideas. Ideas are the step on the stairway that
leads to progress."

"And what progress is?" asked Tommy
Papoulakis. "A car like this one, that's progress.
When you can pay yourself one like this, that is
progress. Do you know what was the idea of man
who invent this little buggy? To catch a beautiful

175

Prayer of the
Young Man
of the Future
Who Is On
His Way
to the City

girl in his town. Like I told you: the sex rule the world. You don't understand that, you don't understand the way world work. Ideas are just to put in books. And I'm not talk about poetry. Put your five gallons of poetry in my tank and see how fast you'll run . . ."

I should have got out. The next time I don't see eye-to-eye with an individual so unpolished, so impermeable to intelligence, I'll take off. Better to travel in an oxcart. This is the last time I'll ever travel in a sports car with a person who sneers at ideas and poetry. Remember what I'm telling You, God, in the event that You can hear me, even though it's impossible because You don't exist.

Finally, we came to the outskirts of the city of Montreal, to a suburb where there were a few trees and a lot of chalets, cabins really, with false bricks covering their walls. The window frames, though, were painted in very bright colours: decoration for brown misery. Suddenly our sports car turned and parked next to one of these shacks.

"Get out with me."

It was a hovel. The stench! Just one room. A bed in one corner. You'd have thought that ten garbage cans had been emptied inside it. In the midst of the mess and the flies, a little man in an undershirt, pale as a ghost, was standing behind a big, fat woman with a slight beard, who hadn't combed her hair since the last snowstorm. On the bed, a big, lazy black dog was sleeping confidently, no doubt because he felt protected by the lady.

I don't know what Tommy Papoulakis said to them. They were conversing in a foreign language. They chatted for a long time. We were standing because the chairs and armchairs were so cluttered. Then, all at once, Tommy pushed open the door. I realized that we were leaving. A cloud of flies that had been buzzing around the room left along with us, rushing into the fresh air. To be polite, I said:

"Goodbye, Madame; goodbye, Monsieur."

The fat woman immediately gave me a tongue-lashing in my language.

"You don't have to say nice things to us.

177

Prayer of the
Young Man
of the Future
Who Is On
His Way
to the City

And don't talk to that wreck of a husband. He pretends he's deaf. He pretends he's got heart trouble too. He's always coughing because he pretends he's got TB. He pretends he's at death's door. He's a heartless man that's always refused to work so he could support me. But when it comes time to eat, he's got a bigger appetite than my big beautiful dog."

Back in the car, we took off again. I didn't know what to say to Tommy Papoulakis. I thought it over a little, then I ventured, cautiously:

"Do they live there?"

"She used to be popular, beautiful singer. My father was abandon his family and his business for that bug. I drop in sometimes to see if he hate her yet. He still love her. She's stop singing and he's turn deaf, but I know for sure he still love her. There's plenty of things in this life we can't understand. You, you think you're Homer. But you've got to learn there's lot of things in life you can't understand unless you know it's the sex that rule the world."

We crossed the bridge that spans the river.

We were surrounded by Montreal, the way sailors say they're surrounded by the ocean, with crowds on the sidewalks and the streets paralyzed by traffic jams.

"Where do you sleep tonight?"

"I don't know yet. I'll figure out something."

"Son of a redheaded whore! This boy wants to reinvent world but doesn't know even where he sleep tonight!"

179

Prayer of the
Young Man
of the Future
Who Is On
His Way
to the City

At the green light, the car leapt across the intersection. Roaring impatiently at every red light, it climbed the street that goes up the mountain. There were as many zigzags as there are on a rabbit path. At last, we pulled up in front of a house that looked like a castle. It could have housed at least fifty young seminarians.

"We don't go any farther today," Tommy Papoulakis announced.

I gathered up my bag.

"Thanks very much, Monsieur."

"Baldheaded son of a redheaded whore! You want to be Prime Minister but you not even try and convince me to invite you inside house . . .

Do you think I let a future Prime Minister to sleep outside like a rake? Come . . ."

We stepped inside. The vestibule, which was as big as our whole house, was decorated with beautiful rich oak panelling, with urns of flowers picked in exotic lands. Tommy Papoulakis announced:

"Laura! I've brought future Prime Minister. Take care of him. He's future of our country and my business!"

And there in her maid's uniform stood our cousin Laura, our mother's first cousin, but not so close to us, because she left our village long before I was born.

Our mother had sent her photographs and she saw the family resemblance right away.

"You must be your mother's oldest. Am I right? Your brother looks more like the other side of the family. Oh, I know about family all right. It's nice of you to come and visit your old cousin! What do you hear from your dear mother?"

During my childhood, our mother often

talked about this cousin in Montreal who was the head servant for a rich family.

"What have you come to Montreal for, you handsome boy?"

"To write poetry."

"It's important to do what you like to do. You can start writing your poetry right away. I'm going to peel the potatoes for Monsieur and Madame's supper."

Now, lying in a big canopy bed that smells like a flower garden, I'm thinking over the day's events. I'm already far from the village where I was born. I feel that the life before me will be interesting. How far will I go?

Even though I've become an unbeliever, I'd like to thank You, God, for the life that You've given me, while You refused it to so many others who will know only nothingness.

181

Prayer of the
Young Man
of the Future
Who Is On
His Way
to the City